THERE'S A
BOY IN
THE GIRLS'
BATHROOM

BOOKS BY LOUIS SACHAR FROM BLOOMSBURY

SERIES FOR YOUNGER READERS

Marvin Redpost series

Wayside School series

THERE'S A BOY IN THE GIRLS' BATHROOM

LOUIS SACHAR

BLOOMSBURY
LONDON OXFORD NEW YORK NEW DELHI SYDNEY

Bloomsbury Publishing, London, Oxford, New York, New Delhi and Sydney

Published in Great Britain in January 2016 by Bloomsbury Publishing Plc
50 Bedford Square, London WC1B 3DP
29 Earlsfort Terrace, Dublin 2, Ireland

First published in the United States of America by
Alfred A. Knopf, Inc., New York

www.bloomsbury.com

BLOOMSBURY, BLOOMSBURY CHILDREN'S BOOKS and the Diana logo are
trademarks of Bloomsbury Publishing Plc

A CIP catalogue record for this book is available from the British Library

ISBN 978 1 4088 6910 9

Printed and bound in Great Britain by CPI Group (UK) Ltd, Croydon CR0 4YY

17

TO CARLA

1.

Bradley Chalkers sat at his desk in the back of the room — last seat, last row. No one sat at the desk next to him or at the one in front of him. He was an island.

If he could have, he would have sat in the closet. Then he could shut the door so he wouldn't have to listen to Mrs. Ebbel. He didn't think she'd mind. She'd probably like it better that way too. So would the rest of the class. All in all, he thought everyone would be much happier if he sat in the closet, but, unfortunately, his desk didn't fit.

"Class," said Mrs. Ebbel. "I would like you all to meet Jeff Fishkin. Jeff has just moved here from Washington, D.C., which, as you know, is our nation's capital."

Bradley looked up at the new kid who was standing at the front of the room next to Mrs. Ebbel.

"Why don't you tell the class a little bit about yourself, Jeff," urged Mrs. Ebbel.

The new kid shrugged.

"There's no reason to be shy," said Mrs. Ebbel.

The new kid mumbled something, but Bradley couldn't hear what it was.

"Have you ever been to the White House, Jeff?" Mrs. Ebbel asked. "I'm sure the class would be very interested to hear about that."

"No, I've never been there," the new kid said very quickly as he shook his head.

Mrs. Ebbel smiled at him. "Well, I guess we'd better find you a place to sit." She looked around the room. "Hmm, I don't see anyplace except, I suppose you can sit there, at the back."

"No, not next to Bradley!" a girl in the front row exclaimed.

"At least it's better than *in front* of Bradley," said the boy next to her.

Mrs. Ebbel frowned. She turned to Jeff. "I'm sorry, but there are no other empty desks."

"I don't mind where I sit," Jeff mumbled.

"Well, nobody likes sitting . . . there," said Mrs. Ebbel.

"That's right," Bradley spoke up. "Nobody likes sitting next to me!" He smiled a strange smile. He stretched his mouth so wide, it was hard to tell whether it was a smile or a frown.

He stared at Jeff with bulging eyes as Jeff awkwardly sat down next to him. Jeff smiled back at him, so he looked away.

As Mrs. Ebbel began the lesson, Bradley took out a pencil and a piece of paper, and scribbled. He scribbled most of the morning, sometimes on the paper and sometimes on his desk. Sometimes he scribbled so hard his pencil point broke. Every time that happened he laughed. Then he'd tape the broken point to one of the gobs of junk in his desk, sharpen his pencil, and scribble again.

4

His desk was full of little wads of torn paper, pencil points, chewed erasers, and other unrecognizable stuff, all taped together.

Mrs. Ebbel handed back a language test. "Most of you did very well," she said. "I was very pleased. There were fourteen A's and the rest B's. Of course, there was one F, but . . ." She shrugged her shoulders.

Bradley held up his test for everyone to see and smiled that same distorted smile.

As Mrs. Ebbel went over the correct answers with the class, Bradley took out his pair of scissors and very carefully cut his test paper into tiny squares.

When the bell rang for recess, he put on his red jacket and walked outside, alone.

"Hey, Bradley, wait up!" somebody called after him.

Startled, he turned around.

Jeff, the new kid, hurried alongside him. "Hi," said Jeff.

Bradley stared at him in amazement.

Jeff smiled. "I don't mind sitting next to you," he said. "Really."

Bradley didn't know what to say.

"I have been to the White House," Jeff admitted. "If you want, I'll tell you about it."

Bradley thought a moment, then said, "Give me a dollar or I'll spit on you."

2.

There are some kids—you can tell just by looking at them—who are good spitters. That is probably the best way to describe Bradley Chalkers. He looked like a good spitter.

He was the oldest and the toughest-looking kid in Mrs. Ebbel's class. He was a year older than the other kids. That was because he had taken the fourth grade twice. Now he was in the fifth grade for the first, but probably not the last, time.

Jeff stared at him, then gave him a dollar and ran away.

Bradley laughed to himself, then watched all the other kids have fun.

When he returned to class after recess, he was surprised Mrs. Ebbel didn't say anything to him. He figured that Jeff would probably tell on him and that he'd have to give back the dollar.

He sat at his desk in the back of the room—last seat, last row. *He's afraid to tell on me,* he decided. *He knows if he tells on me, I'll punch his face in!* He laughed to himself.

He ate lunch alone too.

As he walked in from lunch, Mrs. Ebbel called him to her desk.

"Who, me?" he asked. He glared at Jeff, who was already sitting down. "I didn't do anything."

6

"Did you give my note to your mother?" asked Mrs. Ebbel.

"Huh? What note? You never gave me a note."

Mrs. Ebbel sighed. "Yes I did, Bradley. In fact, I gave you two notes because you said the first one was stolen."

"Oh, that's right," he said. "I gave it to her a long time ago."

Mrs. Ebbel eyed him suspiciously. "Bradley, I think it's very important for your mother to come tomorrow."

Tomorrow was Parents' Conference Day.

"She can't come," said Bradley. "She's sick."

"You never gave her the note, did you?"

"Call her doctor if you don't believe me."

"The school has just hired a new counselor," said Mrs. Ebbel. "And I think it's very important that your mother meet her."

"Oh, they already met," said Bradley. "They go bowling together."

"I'm trying to help you, Bradley."

"Call the bowling alley if you don't believe me!"

"Okay, Bradley," said Mrs. Ebbel, and she let the matter drop.

Bradley returned to his seat, glad that was over. He glanced at Jeff, surprised Jeff hadn't told on him. As he scribbled he kept thinking about what Jeff had said to him. *Hey, Bradley, wait up. Hi. I don't mind sitting next to you. Really. I have been to the White House. If you want, I'll tell you about it.*

It confused him.

He understood it when the other kids were mean to him. It didn't bother him. He simply hated them. As long as he hated them, it didn't matter what they thought of him.

That was why he had threatened to spit on Jeff. He had to hate Jeff before Jeff hated him.

But now he was confused. *Hey, Bradley, wait up. Hi. I don't mind sitting next to you. Really.* The words rolled around in his head and banged against his brain.

After school, he followed Jeff out the door. "Hey, Jeff," he called, "wait up!"

Jeff turned, then started to run, but Bradley was faster. He caught up to Jeff at the corner of the school building.

"I don't have any more money," Jeff said nervously.

"I'll give you a dollar if you'll be my friend," said Bradley. He held out the dollar Jeff had given him earlier.

Jeff slowly reached out, then grabbed it.

Bradley smiled his same twisted smile. "Have you ever been to the White House?" he asked.

"Um . . . yes," said Jeff.

"Me too!" said Bradley. He turned and ran home.

3.

Bradley opened the front door to his house, then made a face. It smelled like fish.

"You're home early," his mother said from the kitchen. She was a large woman with fat arms. She was wearing a sleeveless green dress and holding a butcher knife.

"My friends and me, we raced home," he told her.

A fat fish, about the size of one of Mrs. Chalkers' arms, lay on a board on the counter. Bradley watched her raise the knife above the fish, then quickly hack off its head.

He walked down the hall to his room and closed the door. "Hey, everybody," he announced. "Bradley's home!" But he was pretending that it was someone else who was speaking. "Hi, Bradley. Hi, Bradley," he said.

"Hi, everybody," he answered, this time speaking for himself.

He was talking to his collection of little animals. He had about twenty of them. There was a brass lion that he had found one day in a garbage can on the way to school. There was an ivory donkey that his parents had brought back from their trip to Mexico. There were two owls that were once used as salt and pepper shakers, a glass unicorn with its horn broken, a family

9

of cocker spaniels attached around an ashtray, a raccoon, a fox, an elephant, a kangaroo, and some that were so chipped and broken you couldn't tell what they were. And they were all friends.

And they all liked Bradley.

"Where's Ronnie?" Bradley asked. "And Bartholomew?"

"I don't know," said the fox.

"They're always going off together," said the kangaroo.

Bradley leaned across the bed and reached under his pillow. He pulled out Ronnie the Rabbit and Bartholomew the Bear. He knew they were under his pillow because that was where he had put them before he went to school.

"What were you two doing back there?" he demanded.

Ronnie giggled. She was a little red rabbit with tiny blue eyes glued on her face. One ear was broken. "Nothing, Bradley," she said. "I was just taking a walk."

"Er, I had to go to the bathroom," said Bartholomew. He was a brown-and-white ceramic bear that stood on his hind legs. His mouth was open, revealing beautifully made teeth and a red tongue.

"They were making out!" announced the Mexican donkey. "I saw them kissing!"

Ronnie giggled.

"Oh, Ronnie!" scolded Bradley. "What am I going to do with you?"

10

She giggled again.

Bradley reached into his pocket and took out a handful of cut-up bits of paper, his language test. "Look, everybody," he said. "I brought you some food!" He dropped the bits of paper onto the bed, then scooped all his animals into it. "Not so fast," he said. "There's plenty for everybody."

"Thank you, Bradley," said Ronnie. "It's delicious."

"Yeah, it's real good," said Bartholomew.

"Don't play with your food," the mother cocker spaniel told her three children.

"Pass the salt," said the pepper owl.

"Pass the pepper," said the salt owl.

"Let's hear it for Bradley!" called the lion.

They all cheered, "Yay, Bradley!"

Ronnie finished eating, then hopped off by herself, singing, "doo de-doo de-doo." Then she said, "I think I'll go swimming in the pond."

The pond was a purple stain on Bradley's bedspread where he had once spilled grape juice.

Ronnie jumped into the water. Suddenly she cried, "Help! I have a cramp!"

"You shouldn't have gone swimming right after eating," Bradley reminded her.

"Help! I'm drowning!"

Bartholomew looked up. "That sounds like Ronnie!" he said. "It sounds like she's drowning in the pond!" He hurried to the pond to rescue her. "Hold on, Ronnie!" he shouted. "I'm—"

The door to Bradley's room swung open and his sister, Claudia, barged in. She was four years older than Bradley.

"Get out of here!" he snapped at her. "Or I'll punch your face in!"

"What are you doing?" she teased. "Talking to your little animal friends?" She laughed, showing her braces.

It was Claudia who had broken Ronnie's ear. She had stepped on it accidentally. She told Bradley it was his fault for leaving his animals strewn all over the floor. He didn't tell her that Ronnie wasn't on the floor, but lost in the desert. Instead, he had said, "Who cares? It's just a stupid red rabbit."

"Mom wants you," said Claudia. "She told me to get you."

"What does she want?"

"She wants to talk to you. Tell your animals you'll be right back."

"I wasn't talking to them," Bradley insisted.

"What were you doing then?"

"I was arranging them. I was putting them in alphabetical order. It's a project for school. Call my teacher if you don't believe me."

Claudia snickered. Although she always made fun of Bradley's animals, she had really felt bad when she stepped on the rabbit. She knew it was Bradley's favorite. She had bought him the bear to make up for it. "What do I want a bear for?" he said when she gave it to him.

Bradley went into the kitchen. The fish, now cut

up and covered with onions, was frying on top of the stove. "You want me?" he asked.

"How's everything at school?" asked his mother.

"Great! In fact, today I was elected class president."

"Your grades are all right?"

"Yes. Mrs. Ebbel handed back a language test today and I got another A. In fact, it was an A plus."

"May I see it?"

"Mrs. Ebbel hung it on the wall, next to all my other A tests."

"Mrs. Ebbel just called," said his mother.

His heart fluttered.

"Why didn't you tell me that tomorrow was Parents' Conference Day?" asked his mother.

"Didn't I tell you?" he asked innocently.

"No, I don't think so."

"I told you," he said. "You said you couldn't go. You must have forgot."

"Mrs. Ebbel seems to think it is important for me to be there," said his mother.

"That's just her job," said Bradley. "The more mothers she sees, the more money she makes."

"Well, I made an appointment with her for eleven o'clock tomorrow morning."

Bradley stared at her in disbelief. "No, you can't go!" he shouted, stamping his foot. "It's not fair!"

"Bradley, what—"

"It's not fair! It's not fair!" He ran into his bedroom and slammed the door behind him.

A moment later his mother knocked on the door. "What is it?" she asked. "What's not fair?"

"It's not fair!" he yelled. "You promised!"

"What did I promise? Bradley? What did I promise?"

He didn't answer. He couldn't until he thought up why it wasn't fair and what she had promised him.

He stayed in his room until Claudia told him that he had to come to dinner. He followed her out to the dining room, where his mother and father were already sitting down.

"Did you wash your hands?" asked their father.

"Yes," Bradley and Claudia lied.

Bradley's father worked in the police department. He had been shot in the leg four years ago while chasing a robber. Now he needed a cane to walk, so he worked behind a desk. He didn't like that kind of work and often came home grumpy and short-tempered.

The police never caught the man who had shot him.

"I hate fish," Bradley said as he sat down.

"So do I," said Claudia. "It sticks to my braces and I taste it for weeks."

"Brussels sprouts make me throw up," said Bradley.

"They smell like old garbage," said Claudia.

"That's enough," said their father. "You'll both eat what's on your plates."

Bradley held his nose with one hand while he picked up a brussels sprout with the other, and put it, whole, into his mouth.

"What's all this nonsense about your mother breaking her promise?" asked his father.

Bradley was ready. "She promised she'd take me to the zoo tomorrow, and now she won't!"

"What?" exclaimed his mother. "I never said I'd take you to the zoo."

"She did too!" said Bradley. "Since there is no school tomorrow, she said she'd take me to the zoo."

"I didn't even know there was no school tomorrow until his teacher called me this afternoon," his mother protested.

"You promised!" said Bradley.

"Okay," said his father. "Janet, what time is your appointment tomorrow with Bradley's teacher?"

"Eleven o'clock."

"Okay, you can go to your appointment and still have time to take Bradley to the zoo, after lunch."

"But I never said I'd take him to the zoo."

"You did!" accused Bradley. "And we have to go in the morning. We have to be at the zoo at eleven o'clock!"

Claudia snickered. "Why do you have to be at the zoo at eleven o'clock?"

He glared at her, then turned back to his father. "Because that's when they feed the lions."

Claudia laughed.

"She promised she'd take me to see them feed the lions at eleven o'clock," Bradley insisted.

His mother was flabbergasted. "I—I don't even *know* when they feed the lions!"

"Eleven o'clock," said Bradley.

"Don't lie to your mother," said his father.

"Really," said Bradley. "They feed the lions at eleven o'clock."

"I don't tolerate lying," said his father.

"I'm not lying," said Bradley. "Call the zoo if you don't believe me."

"Don't lie to your mother and don't lie to me!"

"Call the zoo!"

"Your mother said she never promised to take you to the zoo."

"She's lying." Right after he said it, he knew it was a mistake.

His father turned purple with rage. "Don't ever call your mother a liar! Now go to your room!"

"Just call the zoo," Bradley pleaded.

"Maybe I did tell him I'd take him to the zoo," said his mother.

"See!" said Bradley.

"Keep it up, Bradley," said his father. "Just keep it up. You want to be a criminal when you grow up? You want to spend your life in jail? I see people just like you every day at the police station. Just keep it up."

Bradley stared angrily at his father. "Not all criminals go to jail!" he asserted. "What about the man who shot you?"

"I said, go to your room!"

Bradley stood up from the table. "I didn't want to eat this junk anyway." He stomped down the hall into his room and slammed the door. Then he opened it and shouted, "Call the zoo!" one last time, then slammed it again.

He lay on his bed and cried.

"Don't cry, Bradley," said Ronnie. "Everything will be all right."

"You'll think of something, Bradley," said Bartholomew. "You always do. You're the smartest kid in the world."

4.

Bradley stood at the front door and hollered, "Mrs. Ebbel is a liar! Don't believe anything she tells you."

Bradley's mother got into the car, gritted her teeth, and drove to school. She was just as afraid as Bradley, if not more so, of what Mrs. Ebbel would tell her.

She wanted to believe Bradley when he told her he was getting all A's or was elected class president. She tried to fool herself that it could be true, even though she knew it couldn't. She knew her son. And she knew Mrs. Ebbel wouldn't take the trouble to call her on the phone if everything were really as wonderful as Bradley said it was. Still, she hoped.

She opened the door to Bradley's classroom. No one was there. "Hello?" she called out timidly.

She looked around. There was a bulletin board covered with A papers. She looked from one paper to another and hoped, with all her heart, that she'd see one with Bradley's name on it. She didn't.

In the back corner of the room she saw a chart that listed the name of every student in the class. Next to each name was a row of gold stars. Next to "Bradley Chalkers," there were no stars.

"Mrs. Chalkers?"

Startled, she turned around to see Mrs. Ebbel. "Oh, you scared me," she said, then smiled.

Mrs. Ebbel didn't smile.

Mrs. Chalkers sat at a chair next to the teacher's desk and bravely listened as Mrs. Ebbel told her about Bradley. There was nothing Mrs. Ebbel said that she didn't already know. Still, it hurt to hear it.

"Deep down, he really is a good boy," she tried to tell Bradley's teacher.

"I'm sure he has a lot of good qualities," said Mrs. Ebbel. "However, I have twenty-eight other children in my class, and I can't spend all my time trying to help Bradley. He has to decide whether he wants to be a part of the class or not. And if he doesn't want to be a part of the class, then he shouldn't be here. He just makes it that much harder for everyone else."

"What can I do?" asked Bradley's mother.

"The school has just hired a counselor," said Mrs. Ebbel. "I'd like your permission for Bradley to begin seeing her once a week."

"Anything that will help my son," said Mrs. Chalkers.

"I don't know if she can help him or not," said Mrs. Ebbel. "Bradley has a very serious behavior problem. If he doesn't show improvement soon, more drastic measures will have to be taken."

"Deep down, he really is a good boy," said Bradley's mother.

"Well, let's go meet the counselor," said Mrs. Ebbel. She led Bradley's mother down the halls to the counselor's office. The door was open, but no one was there.

Bradley's mother stepped into the room. Boxes were everywhere. Some were turned over, with their contents half spilled onto the floor. A yellow ladder lay on its side. In the center of the room was a round table surrounded by chairs, but the table and chairs were covered with papers and boxes and games and books. There was hardly room for Bradley's mother and teacher to stand.

"She's just moving in," Mrs. Ebbel explained. "I'm sure she'll have it cleaned up by tomorrow."

Mrs. Chalkers shrugged. She picked up a dolphin puppet from an open box on the table and put her hand inside it.

Suddenly there was a loud grunt and a young woman entered the room. She dropped the box she was carrying, and more than a hundred crayons spilled out across the floor. "Oh, hello," she said.

She was a lot younger than either Mrs. Ebbel or Mrs. Chalkers. She wore blue jeans and a red T-shirt with ROCK 'N' ROLL written across it in light blue letters. She had light brown hair, almost blond, and clear blue eyes.

"I'm Carla Davis," she said, and held out her hand.

Bradley's mother stared at her a moment, then reached out to shake her hand but suddenly realized she was still wearing the dolphin puppet. She quickly removed it and put it back in the box on the table.

The counselor smiled.

"She needs to sign the form so that you can start seeing her son," said Mrs. Ebbel.

Miss Davis looked hopelessly around her office. "They're around here somewhere," she muttered, then began tearing into the boxes.

"Perhaps I'd better come back," said Bradley's mother.

"Found them!" said the counselor, holding up the forms. She cleared a space on the round table by pushing away a box and gave Mrs. Chalkers a form to sign.

Bradley's mother looked around the messy office, then at the young woman with the rock 'n' roll T-shirt. She shrugged her shoulders and signed her name.

Miss Davis took the form from her. "Oh! You're Bradley Chalkers' mother!"

Mrs. Chalkers nodded.

"You would not believe all the horror stories I've heard about Bradley Chalkers," said the new counselor. "I've been here less than three hours but it seems like every teacher in the school has dropped by to warn me about him."

"Deep down, he really is—" Bradley's mother started to say.

"I can't wait to meet him," the counselor interrupted. "He sounds charming, just delightful."

5.

At dinner Bradley's father asked how the meeting with Bradley's teacher went.

Bradley looked down at his mashed potatoes.

"Fine," said his mother. "Bradley is doing very well."

"Good. Glad to hear it," said his father.

Bradley was glad to hear it too.

Later that evening his mother came into his room. "I met Miss Davis, the new counselor," she said. "You're going to begin seeing her tomorrow."

"No," said Bradley. "I won't go!"

"Please, Bradley. Don't be that way. She can help you, if you'll let her."

"I don't need any help. You said I was doing very well."

"Did you want me to tell your father the truth? Do you want to be sent to military school? Maybe he's right. I don't know. Maybe that's what you need."

"You said I was doing very well. I heard you."

"Please, Bradley," said his mother. "Give Miss Davis a chance. *Please.*"

"You should have taken me to the zoo."

It was drizzling the next morning as Bradley walked to school. He wore red rubber boots and a yellow raincoat. He stamped in every puddle along the way, making big splashes.

He suddenly stopped when he saw Jeff standing next to the school, under the overhang. Bradley's right foot remained in the center of a puddle as he stared at his one and only friend.

He took a deep breath, then slowly walked toward Jeff. "He has to like me," he tried to convince himself. "I gave him a dollar."

"Hi, Bradley," Jeff greeted him.

He didn't answer.

"If you want, I can help you with your homework sometimes," Jeff offered. "I know I'm new here, but I'm pretty smart, and we learned the same stuff at my old school." He shrugged modestly.

Bradley looked at Jeff as if he were from outer space. "I don't need any help," he said. "I'm the smartest kid in class. Ask anyone."

They headed for Mrs. Ebbel's room, side by side but not necessarily together.

6.

Jeff Fishkin was hopelessly lost. He clutched his hall pass as he looked down the long empty corridor. The school seemed so big to him.

He was on his way to see the new counselor. She was supposed to help him "adjust to his new environment." Now he not only didn't know how to get to her office, he had no idea how to get back to Mrs. Ebbel's class either.

The floor was slippery. It had started raining during recess and the kids had tracked water and mud inside with them.

A teacher carrying a stack of papers stepped out of a door and Jeff hurried up to her. "Can you tell me where the counselor's office is, please?" he asked. His voice trembled.

The teacher first checked to make sure he had a hall pass. Then she said: "The counselor's office . . . let's see. Go down this hall to the end, turn right, and it's the third door on your left."

"Thank you very much," said Jeff. He started to go.

"No, wait," said the teacher. "That's not right, she's in the new office in the other wing. Turn around and go back the way you just came, then turn left at the end of the hall and it's the second door on your right."

"Thank you," Jeff said again.

He walked to the end of the hall, turned right, counted to the second door on his left, and pushed it open.

A girl with red hair and a freckled face was washing her hands at the sink. When she saw Jeff, her mouth dropped open. "What are you doing in here?" she asked.

"Huh?" Jeff uttered.

"Get out of here!" she yelled. "This is the girls' bathroom!"

Jeff froze. He covered his face with his hands, then dashed out the door.

"THERE'S A BOY IN THE GIRLS' BATH-ROOM!" the girl screamed after him.

He raced down the hall. Suddenly his feet slipped out from under him. He waved his arms wildly as he tried to keep his balance, then flopped down on the floor.

"Oh no, no, no, oh no, no, no," he groaned. "What have I done? Oh, why didn't I just read the sign on the door? This is the worst day of my whole life!"

Suddenly he realized he was no longer holding the hall pass. He stood up and frantically looked around. "Don't tell me I dropped it in the girls' bathroom."

He heard someone coming and hurried off in the opposite direction. He rounded the corner, then spotted what looked like some kind of storage room. It was cluttered with boxes.

He ducked inside and closed the door behind him.

"Hello," said a voice.

He spun around.

A woman stepped down off a yellow ladder. "You must be Jeff," she said. "I'm Carla Davis." She smiled and held out her hand. "I'm so glad you've come. I was afraid you might get lost."

7.

Jeff sat at the round table. The counselor sat across from him.

"So how do you like Red Hill School?" she asked.

He stared straight ahead. *There's a boy in the girls' bathroom* echoed inside his head.

"I imagine it must seem a little scary," said the counselor.

He didn't answer.

"I think it's scary," she said. "It seems so big! Anytime I try to go anywhere, I get lost."

He smiled weakly.

"It's hard for me because I'm new here," she explained. "Today is only my second day of school. I don't know anybody. Nobody knows me. The other teachers all look at me strangely. It's hard for me to make friends with them. They already have their own friends."

"I know what you mean," Jeff said.

"Maybe you can help me," said the counselor.

"Me?" said Jeff. "How can *I* help *you*? I'm the one who needs help!"

"Well, maybe we can help each other. What do you think about that?"

"How?"

"We're the two new kids at school," she said. "We

can share our experiences and learn from each other."

Jeff smiled. "Okay, Miss Davis," he said.

"Jeff," she said, "if we're going to be friends, I want you to call me Carla, not Miss Davis."

He laughed.

"Do you think Carla is a funny name?"

"Oh, no! I just never called a teacher by her first name, that's all."

"But we're friends. Friends don't call each other Miss Davis and Mr. Fishkin, do they?"

Jeff laughed again. "No," he said, then he frowned. "The kids in my class call me Fishface."

"Have you made any friends?" asked Carla.

"I sort of made one friend," said Jeff, "but I don't like him."

"How can he be your friend if you don't like him?"

"Nobody likes him. At first I felt sorry for him because nobody wanted to sit next to him. Mrs. Ebbel said it out loud right in front of the whole class. 'Nobody likes sitting there,' she said. It was like he wasn't even there. It's bad enough when a kid says something like that, but a teacher."

"It must have hurt his feelings," said Carla.

"No. He just smiled."

"He may have been smiling on the outside, but do you think he really was smiling on the inside?"

"I don't know. I guess not. I guess that's why I tried to be friends with him. I told him I liked sitting next to him. But then he said, 'Give me a dollar or I'll spit on you.'"

"What did you do?"

"I gave him a dollar. I didn't want him to spit on me. But then, later, he said, 'I'll give you a dollar to be my friend.' So I took it. It was my dollar! So does that mean I have to be his friend, even though I just broke even?"

"What do you think friendship is?" Carla asked him.

"I don't know. I mean I know what it is, but I can't explain it."

"Is it something you can buy and sell? Can you go to the store and get a quart of milk, a dozen eggs, and a friend?"

Jeff laughed. "No. So does that mean I don't have to be friends with him?"

"I won't tell you what to do," said Carla. "All I can do is help you think for yourself."

"I don't even know if Bradley wants to be my friend," said Jeff. "Today, at recess, we hung around together but we didn't do anything. He acted like I wasn't there. Then, when it started to rain, he ran around trying to push little kids into the mud."

"Could you share your feelings with him?" asked Carla. "That's the real way to build a friendship: by talking, and by being honest and by sharing your feelings. Like the way we're talking and being honest with each other now. That's why we're friends."

"But Bradley's different than you and me," said Jeff.

"I think you'll find that if you're nice to Bradley,

he'll be nice to you. If you are honest and friendly with him, he'll be honest and friendly with you. It's just like with the dollar. You always break even."

Jeff smiled. "Are you going to see Bradley, too?" he asked.

"Yes, later today."

"Do you think you'll be able to help him?"

"I don't know."

"I hope so. I think he needs help even more than me. You won't tell him anything I said, will you?"

"No, that's one of my most important rules. I never repeat anything anyone tells me here, around the round table."

"Never?"

She shook her head.

"What about to other teachers?"

She shook it again.

"What about to the principal?"

"Nope."

"Okay," said Jeff. He took a breath. "Here goes." He grimaced. "On the way here, I got a little lost, and, um, accidentally went into the girls' bathroom!" He covered his face with his hands.

8.

Mrs. Ebbel was teaching geography. Everybody in the class had a map of the United States on his or her desk.

Bradley's map was different from all the others. California was above Wisconsin. Florida stuck out of Texas. He picked up his pair of scissors and carefully cut out Tennessee. He was a good cutter. The edge of his scissors never left the black line.

He wondered what was happening to Jeff. He knew he was at the counselor's office. He imagined she was doing all kinds of horrible things to him. He had tried to tell Jeff at recess not to go see her.

He taped Tennessee to Washington. He was a very messy taper. His piece of tape twisted and stuck to itself.

He looked up as Jeff entered the room and watched him hang the hall pass on the hook behind Mrs. Ebbel's desk. Then he looked away as Jeff headed for the seat next to him.

When the bell rang for lunch, he shoved his map into his desk and pulled out his paper sack. Because of the rain, everyone had to eat inside, in the auditorium. He and Jeff walked there together—sort of. *He's walking next to me*, Bradley thought, *but I'm not walking next to him.*

The auditorium was hot, steamy, and noisy. Long tables with benches had been set up across the room.

"Where do you want to sit?" asked Jeff.

Bradley ignored him. He stood on his tiptoes and looked around the room as if he was trying to locate his real friends.

Jeff walked away and sat at one of the tables.

Bradley walked behind where Jeff was sitting. "Hmm, I think I'll sit here," he said aloud, as if he didn't know Jeff was there. He stepped over the bench and sat down next to him.

"Hi," said Jeff.

Bradley faced him for the first time. "Oh, it's you," he said.

They ate their lunches.

"What are you eating?" asked Jeff.

"Peanubudder sandige," said Bradley. As he spoke, bits of peanut butter and bread flew from his mouth. "Wha' bou' you?"

"Tuna fish," said Jeff.

Bradley swallowed his food and said, "I hate tuna fish."

"My mother makes it good," said Jeff. "She chops apples in it."

"I hate apples," said Bradley. He sucked the last drop of milk through his straw, then continued to suck, making a gurgling noise.

Sitting two tables away from Jeff and Bradley were three girls; Melinda Birch, Lori Westin, and Colleen

32

Verigold. They were talking and laughing about something funny that had happened to Colleen that morning.

Colleen, who had red hair and a freckled face, covered her mouth with her hand. "There he is!" she whispered. "It's him!"

"Where?" asked Lori

"Don't look at him!" said Colleen. "He's right there, sitting next to Bradley Chalkers."

"Bradley Chalkers," said Lori. "I think I'm going to throw up!"

"Don't look," whispered Colleen.

Bradley stopped sucking on his straw. "What'd the counselor do to you?" he asked.

Jeff shrugged. "Nothing."

"Did she yell a lot? Was she mean and ugly?"

"No. She was nice. I think you'll like her."

"*Me?*" asked Bradley. "I'm not going to see her. I didn't do anything wrong."

"She's good at helping you solve your problems," said Jeff.

"I don't have any problems," said Bradley. He bit ferociously into a red delicious apple.

"I thought you said you hated apples," said Jeff.

Bradley shoved the apple back inside the paper sack. "That wasn't an apple," he said. "It was a banana."

Jeff's face suddenly changed color, first white, then bright red.

"Ooh, I think he sees you," said Melinda.

Lori laughed.

Colleen blushed.

"C'mon," said Lori. "Let's go talk to him." She stood up. Lori Westin was a short, skinny girl with long straight black hair.

Melinda got up from the table too. She was nearly twice the size of Lori. She had short brown hair.

"No, don't go!" pleaded Colleen.

"What's the matter?" asked Bradley.

"Uh, nothing," said Jeff. "So, did I miss anything in class?"

"No. Mrs. Ebbel gave everybody a map."

"I got one."

"Don't lose it," said Bradley. "Mrs. Ebbel wants them back."

Two girls were giggling behind them.

Jeff and Bradley turned around.

"Colleen thinks you're cute," said Lori.

Jeff blushed. "Who?" he asked.

The girls laughed.

"What's your name?" asked Melinda.

Jeff blushed again.

"*Colleen* wants to know," said Lori, then she and Melinda laughed again.

"He doesn't have a name!" said Bradley, coming to Jeff's rescue. He hated Lori. She had the biggest mouth in the whole school. She was always laughing, too. He could hear her laugh from one end of the school to the other.

"E-uuu, Bradley Chalkers!" said Lori, holding her nose.

"Lori Loudmouth!" said Bradley.

"We're not talking to you, Bradley," said Melinda.

"Get out of here or I'll punch your face in," he replied.

"You wouldn't hit a girl," said Melinda.

"That's what you think." He shook his fist.

Melinda and Lori backed away. "We only wanted to know his name," said Melinda.

"And what he was doing in the girls' bathroom!" screeched Lori.

The two girls laughed and ran back to Colleen. Bradley slowly turned and looked at Jeff, amazed. Jeff sat with his head on the table and his arms over his head.

"You went into the girls' bathroom?" Bradley asked.

"So what?" said Jeff from under his elbow. "Carla says—"

"Me too!" declared Bradley. "I go all the time! I like to make them scream!"

He smiled at Jeff.

9.

"Bradley Chalkers! What are you doing out of class?"

It was a teacher. Bradley didn't know her, but it seemed as though every teacher in the school knew him. "I got a hall pass!" he told her.

"Let me see it."

He showed it to her. "Mrs. Ebbel gave it to me. Go ask her if you don't believe me."

"Where are you going?"

"Library," he said. "To get a book."

"Okay, but make sure you go straight to the library. No detours, Bradley."

He had lied. He wasn't even allowed to check books out of the library.

The door to the counselor's office was open, so he walked right in. "I'm here," he announced. "Whadda ya want?"

Carla smiled warmly at him. "Hello, Bradley," she said. "I'm Carla Davis. It's a pleasure to see you today." She held out her hand. "I've been looking forward to meeting you."

He was amazed by how young and pretty she was. He had been expecting an ugly old hag.

She had sky-blue eyes and soft blond hair. She wore a white shirt covered with different-colored squiggly lines, like some kid had scribbled on it. But as he stared at the shirt he realized that it was made to look that way, on purpose.

"Aren't you going to shake my hand?" she asked.

"No, you're too ugly." He walked past her and sat down at the round table.

She sat across from him. "I appreciate your coming to see me," she said.

"I had to come. Mrs. Ebbel made me."

"For whatever reason, I'm glad you came."

"I meant to go to the library," he explained. "I came here by accident."

"Oh, I don't believe in accidents," said Carla.

"You don't believe in accidents?" That was the craziest thing he'd ever heard.

She shook her head.

"What about when you spill your milk?"

"Do you like milk?" asked Carla.

"No, I hate it!"

"So maybe you spill it on purpose," she said. "You just think it's an accident." She smiled.

He stared angrily down at the table. He felt like he'd been tricked. "I don't drink milk," he said. "I drink coffee."

He glanced around the room. It was full of all kinds of interesting-looking objects. "This place is a mess," he said.

"I know," Carla admitted. "I like messy rooms. Clean rooms are boring and depressing. They remind me of hospitals."

"Don't you get in trouble?"

"Why should I?"

He didn't know the answer to that. But he knew that if it were his room and it was this messy, he'd get in trouble. "I didn't do anything wrong!" he declared.

"Nobody said you did."

"Well, then how come I have to be here?"

"I was hoping you'd like it here," said Carla. "I was hoping we could be friends. Do you think we can?"

"No."

"Why not?"

"Because I don't like you."

"I like you," said Carla. "I can like you, can't I? You don't have to like me."

He squirmed in his seat.

"I was also hoping you'd be able to teach me things," said Carla.

"You're the teacher, not me."

"So? That doesn't matter. A teacher can often learn a lot more from a student than a student can learn from a teacher."

"I've taught Mrs. Ebbel a lot," Bradley agreed. "Today I taught her geography."

"What do you want to teach me?" Carla asked.

"What do you want to know?"

"You tell me," said Carla. "What's the most important thing you can teach me?"

Bradley tried to think of something he knew. "The elephant's the biggest animal in the world," he said. "But it's afraid of mice."

"I wonder why that is," said Carla.

"Because," said Bradley, "if a mouse ran up an elephant's trunk, it would get stuck and then the elephant wouldn't be able to breathe and so it would die. That's how most elephants die."

"I see," said Carla. "Thank you for sharing that with me. You're a very good teacher."

He suddenly felt like he'd been tricked again. He didn't want to share anything with her. He hated her.

"What else do you want to teach me?" she asked.

"Nothing," he said coldly. "You're not supposed to talk in school."

"Why not?"

"It's a rule. Like no sticking gum in the water fountains."

"Well, in this room there are no rules," said Carla. "In here, everyone thinks for himself. No one tells you what to do."

"You mean I can stick gum in the water fountain?"

"You could, except I don't have a water fountain."

"Can I break something?" he asked.

"Certainly."

He looked around for something to break, then caught himself in time. It was another trick. He'd break something and then get in trouble, and nobody would believe him when he said that she had said there were no rules. "I'm not in the mood," he said.

"All right, but if you are ever in the mood, there are a lot of things you can break—things I like very much and things that other children use."

"I will!" he assured her. "I know karate." He raised his hand sideways over the table. "I can break this table in half with my bare hand."

"I'd hate to see you hurt your hand."

"Nothing ever hurts me," he told her. "I've broken every table in my house," he declared. "The chairs, too. Call my mother if you don't believe me."

"I believe you," said Carla. "Why shouldn't I?"

"You should."

She did, too. For the rest of the meeting, no matter what he told her, she believed him.

When he told her that his parents only fed him dog food, she asked him how it tasted.

"Delicious!" he said. "Meaty and sweet."

"I've always wanted to try it," said Carla.

When he told her that the President had called him on the phone last night, she asked what they talked about.

"Hats," he answered right away.

"Hats? What did you say about hats?"

"I asked him why he didn't wear a hat like Abraham Lincoln."

"And what did he say?"

Bradley thought a moment. "I can't tell you. It's top secret."

Near the end of the session, Carla gave him a piece of construction paper and asked him if he wanted to draw a picture. He chose a black crayon from the big box of crayons and stayed with it the whole time. He scribbled wildly all over the paper.

Carla leaned over to look at it. "That's very nice," she said.

"It's a picture of nighttime," he told her.

"Oh. I thought it was a picture of the floor of a barber shop, after someone with black curly hair got his hair cut."

"That's what it is!" Bradley declared. "That's what I meant."

"It's very good," said Carla. "May I have it?"

"What for?"

"I'd like to hang it up on my wall."

He looked at her in amazement. "You mean here?"

"Yes."

"No, it's mine."

"I was hoping you'd share it with me," said Carla.

"It costs a dollar."

"It's worth it," said Carla. "But I only want it if you're willing to share it."

"No," he said.

"Okay, but if you ever change your mind, I'll still want it."

"You can make me give it to you," he suggested.

"No, I can't."

"Sure you can. Teachers make kids do things all the time."

Carla shook her head.

It was time for him to return to class.

"I've enjoyed your visit very much," said Carla. "Thank you for sharing so much with me." She held out her hand.

He backed away from it as if it were some kind of poisonous snake. Then he turned and hurried out into the hall.

When he got to Mrs. Ebbel's class, he crumpled his picture into a ball and dropped it in the wastepaper basket next to her desk.

10.

Bradley sat at his desk in the back of the room. Last seat, last row. He felt safe there. The counselor had scared him. She was even worse than he had imagined.

He looked at Jeff, who smiled at him and then returned to his work.

Bradley was glad Jeff was his friend. *Jeff and me are a lot alike*, he thought. *We're both smart. We both hate the counselor. And we both like sneaking into girls' bathrooms.*

Actually, Bradley never had been inside a girls' bathroom. It was something he'd always wanted to do, but he'd never had the courage even to peek into one. But now that he and Jeff were friends, he hoped Jeff would take him inside one. He was dying to know what they looked like.

He imagined they were carpeted in gold, with pink wallpaper and red velvet toilet seats. He thought girl toilets would look nothing like boy toilets. They'd probably be more like fountains, with colored water.

"So, how'd you like Carla?" Jeff asked him after school. They were walking along the sidewalk next to the school building, carrying their raincoats. It was no longer raining.

"She's we-ird!" he replied. "She likes to eat dog food!"

Jeff made a face. "Did she say that?"

Bradley nodded. "She asked me why the President doesn't wear a hat! How am I supposed to know that?"

Jeff shrugged and said, "I don't know."

"You don't like her, do you?" Bradley asked.

"She's o—"

"I hate her!" said Bradley.

"Me too," said Jeff. "I hate her!"

Bradley smiled his distorted smile. "You want to go sneak inside the girls' bathroom?" he asked.

"You mean now?"

"Why not?"

"Um, now's not a good time," said Jeff.

"Why not?"

Jeff thought a moment. "There won't be any girls there now," he said. "They all go home to use their own bathrooms."

"You're right," Bradley agreed. "Good thinking. We'll do it tomorrow during recess."

Jeff smiled weakly.

They walked around the corner of the building.

"Hello, Jeff," said Lori Westin.

"Hi, Jeff," said Melinda Birch.

"Hi, J—" Colleen said so quietly that the "eff" couldn't be heard.

They'd been waiting for him to come by. Somehow they had found out his name.

"Hello, hi, hi," Jeff answered, blushing.

Lori laughed. Then the three girls hurried away.

"Stupid girls," said Bradley.

"Yeah," Jeff muttered.

"I hate them!" said Bradley.

"Me too!" said Jeff.

"Why'd you say hello to them?"

"They said hello to me, first," Jeff replied.

"So?"

Jeff shrugged. "Whenever anybody says hello to me, I always say hello back."

"Why?"

"I don't know. I can't help it. It's like when someone says 'thank you.' Don't you automatically say 'you're welcome'?"

"No."

"I do," said Jeff. He shrugged again. "I guess it's like a reflex. Like when you go to the doctor and he taps your knee, you have to kick. You can't help it. It's the same thing. When someone says hello to me, I always have to say hello back."

Bradley tried to make sense out of what Jeff said. "I know what you can do," he suggested. "The next time one of those girls says hello to you—kick her!"

11.

A week later they still hadn't gone into the girls' bathroom. Jeff always had a good reason why it wasn't the right time. Recess was the wrong time, because it would be better to wait until after lunch, after the girls had eaten. Lunch was no good, because they hadn't had time to digest their food. Listening to Jeff, it would seem that girls *never* had to go to the bathroom.

But Bradley had never been happier. He was thrilled to have a friend. He even was beginning to like school.

Jeff had two gold stars next to his name. Bradley felt proud when he looked at them, almost like he had earned them himself.

"What do you want to do?" Jeff asked.

"Nothing," said Bradley.

It was lunchtime. They had finished eating and were sitting out on the grass.

"Did the counselor say anything stupid today?" Bradley asked.

Jeff hesitated. He looked down at the ground, then boldly stated, "I like her."

Bradley was shocked.

"She said that I can like her even if you hate her," Jeff asserted. "It doesn't mean that you and I can't still be friends. We don't have to agree on everything. She said friendships are stronger when everyone has different opinions to share."

"You told her I hated her?" Bradley asked.

Jeff nodded.

"Good."

"Except she didn't believe me," said Jeff.

"She's weird," said Bradley. "She never believes anything anyone says. I'm not going to see her anymore."

"She said you don't have to. I told her you wouldn't show up today and she said that was okay. She said you don't have to do anything you don't want to do."

Bradley turned and looked back toward the school, in the direction of the counselor's office. "That's one of her tricks," he said.

"So what do you want to do?" Jeff asked.

"Nothing."

A basketball bounced away from the basketball court and rolled toward them. Jeff jumped up and grabbed it.

"Hey, Fishnose, over here!" called Robbie, a boy from their class.

"Kick it the other way," urged Bradley.

Jeff threw the ball all the way on a fly to Robbie.

"You should have kicked it onto the roof," said Bradley.

"Maybe they'll let us play," said Jeff. "Let's ask them."

Bradley shook his head. "No, I don't want to."

Jeff watched the boys play basketball for a moment, then sat back down with Bradley.

"Uh-oh," Bradley said. "Here come those girls again. Try not to say hello to them."

"Hello, Jeff," said Lori.

"Hello," said Jeff.

"Hi," said Melinda.

"Hi," said Jeff.

"Hi, Jeff," whispered Colleen.

"Hi," whispered Jeff.

Lori laughed as the three girls walked away.

Jeff shrugged. "I can't help it," he said sadly.

"Let's go beat them up!" said Bradley. "Then they won't say hello to you anymore." He started after them, but Jeff didn't follow. "C'mon," Bradley urged. "Girls are easy to beat up. You just have to hit them once, and they cry and run away."

"Not now," said Jeff.

"Why not?"

"Everyone will see us. We'll get in trouble."

Bradley stopped. "You're right," he agreed. "We'll get them after school."

"I can't," said Jeff. "I've got to go right home after school and do my homework."

Bradley was beginning to get fed up. "How come you're always doing your *homework?*" he asked, hands on hips. He said the word *homework* the way other people might say the word *manure*.

Jeff shrugged.

"Do you like doing it?" Bradley asked.

"It's okay. I don't mind too much."

Bradley kicked at the ground. "Do you think if I did my homework, Mrs. Ebbel might give me a gold star?" he asked.

"I don't think she gives gold stars just for doing homework," said Jeff. "But she might!"

"Maybe I should do it sometime," said Bradley.

"Why don't you come over after school today?" Jeff asked. "We can do our homework together."

Bradley's face twisted in anguish. "Today? I don't think today's a good day to do homework."

"I can help y—" Jeff started to say, then stopped. "You can help me with the stuff I don't understand."

"All right!" said Bradley. "I'll do it!"

"Good!" said Jeff.

"First, we'll beat up those girls," said Bradley, "then we'll go to your house and do our homework."

12.

Just before the end of the lunch period, someone knocked very lightly on the door to the counselor's office.

"Come in," said Carla.

A girl timidly stepped inside. "Are you Miss Davis?" she asked.

"Yes, but I prefer to be called Carla."

"Do I have to tell you my name?" asked the girl.

"No, not if you don't want to."

"Colleen Verigold," said the girl. She sat down in one of the chairs around the round table and said, "I don't know who to invite to my birthday party."

Carla remained standing.

"See, there's this boy I want to invite," said Colleen. "Do I have to tell you his name?"

"No."

"Jeff Fishkin."

Carla smiled.

"But if I invite Jeff, then I'll have to invite another boy, because I can't invite seven girls and only one boy, can I?"

"I don't—"

"Except Jeff has only one friend and he's the most horrible, rotten boy in the whole school! I can't invite Bradley Chalkers to my birthday party, I just can't!" She took a breath. "So what should I do?"

"You want *me* to tell you whom to invite to *your* birthday party?"

"Lori says you're good at solving problems."

"Lori solves her own problems. I just help her think for herself."

"But I don't know what to think!" Colleen exclaimed. "I can't invite seven girls and only one boy. And I can't invite Bradley!"

"When's your birthday?"

"November thirteenth."

"Then you still have plenty of time," said Carla. "Let me give you a form for your parents to sign. Right now, I'm not even allowed to talk to you without your parents' permission."

"That's dumb!"

"No it isn't," said Carla. "Some parents don't want strangers giving advice to their children."

"But my parents won't care," said Colleen. "They said I can invite anybody I want to my birthday party."

"That's not the point," said Carla. She handed her the form.

Colleen reluctantly took it. "Can't you just whisper it to me?" she asked.

Carla shook her head.

Melinda and Lori were waiting for Colleen when she came out. "Who are you going to invite?" asked Melinda.

"Not Bradley," said Lori. "*Please,* not Bradley."

"I don't know yet," said Colleen. "She won't tell me until my parents sign this form."

13.

Bradley dragged his feet as he walked to Carla's office.

She was waiting in the hall for him. "It's a pleasure to see you today," she said. "I appreciate your coming to see me." She held out her hand.

He stepped past her and sat down at the round table. She sat across from him.

"The reason the President doesn't wear a hat is because the doorways are too low," he said. "He used to wear one, but every time he walked through a door, he'd hit his hat and it would fall on the floor."

"That makes sense," Carla agreed. "Thank you for sharing that with me. But," she whispered, "I thought you weren't allowed to tell me such top secret information."

"The President says he trusts you," said Bradley.

"Thank you, Bradley," said Carla. "I'm glad you trust me."

He looked at her as if he thought she were deaf. He hadn't said *he* trusted her. He had said the *President* trusted her, but he decided to let it go.

She was wearing a yellow shirt with large green triangular buttons all the way down the front. On one side of the buttons was a big white exclamation point. On the other side, there was a big white question mark.

"Jeff trusts you too," he said.

"I understand you two have become friends," said Carla.

"We're best friends."

"That's wonderful," said Carla.

"Today, after school, we're going to do our homework together. At his house! I'm going to help him with the stuff he doesn't understand."

"That's very nice of you," said Carla. "I'm sure Jeff appreciates having you as a friend."

"I'm his only friend," said Bradley.

"But even if he had other friends—"

"He won't have any other friends," Bradley interrupted.

"You don't know that."

"Yes I do. I'm his only friend."

"But suppose he makes new friends?"

"I don't want him to."

"But if he made new friends, then his new friends could become your friends too."

"He won't," said Bradley, shaking his head.

"Just because you and he are friends, that doesn't mean he can't have other friends too," said Carla.

"Yes it does."

"Why?"

"Because," he said proudly. "So long as Jeff is friends with me, nobody else will like him!"

14.

Homework. After school Bradley Chalkers was going to go to Jeff Fishkin's house, and they were going to do their homework together. Bradley couldn't believe it. *Homework.* It was all he thought about as he sat at his desk—last seat, last row—and waited for school to end. *Maybe it won't be too horrible,* he reasoned. *After all, Jeff always does his homework. He must like it.*

The more he thought about it, the more he liked the idea. *Homework: Work you do at home.* Except he wouldn't do it at his home, he would do it at Jeff's home, and that was even better. It would be his first time over at Jeff's house.

And after he did his homework, Mrs. Ebbel might give him a gold star. Instead of scribbling, he drew little stars, one after another until the bell rang.

But first they had to beat up those girls.

"C'mon, let's go," he said, hopping out of his seat.

"Just a sec," said Jeff. He got a book from his desk.

"Oh, do I need one of those?" Bradley asked. He hadn't realized that in order to do his homework, he would need to bring his book home.

"That's okay, we can share mine."

They walked outside. There was a light drizzle.

"They're in Mrs. Sharp's class," said Bradley. "We

can wait here until they come out, then sneak up behind them."

"Who?"

"Those girls. We have to beat them up so they won't say hello to you."

"We should probably get started on our homework right away," said Jeff.

"It won't take long," Bradley assured him. "You just have to hit them once, and they cry and run away."

"But it's raining," said Jeff. It was barely misting.

"Good! We can push them in the mud and get their clothes dirty. Girls hate it when their clothes get dirty."

They stood about ten yards away from Mrs. Sharp's door and waited. Several kids came out, but they didn't see Colleen, Lori, or Melinda.

"Maybe they've already gone home," Jeff said hopefully.

"No, girls always take a long time to leave class," Bradley explained. "First, they have to put their papers *neatly* in their notebooks. Then they have to mark their places in their books and put all their pencils in their pencil holders. Then they put everything away, *neatly*, in their desks." He said it as though it was the most disgusting thing anyone could do. "Shh! Here they come."

Melinda, followed by Colleen and Lori, came out of Mrs. Sharp's room.

Bradley put his finger to his lips, then he and Jeff

walked after them, keeping their distance. They followed the girls around the side of the building and along the sidewalk away from the school.

"Let's just go home," said Jeff. "The homework might take a long time."

"Girls kick," warned Bradley. "They don't know how to punch, so they try to kick you." He quickened his pace until he was just a few steps behind the girls. Jeff lagged a little behind.

Lori was the first to turn around. "E-uuu, Bradley Chalkers!" she said, making a face.

"Lori Loudmouth," snapped Bradley. "The ugliest girl in school!"

Melinda and Colleen stopped walking and turned around too.

"Grow up, Bradley," said Melinda.

"Make me," he replied.

"Hello, Jeff," Colleen said very quietly.

"Hello," said Jeff.

"Quit saying hello to him!" said Bradley.

"It's a free country," said Lori. "We can say hello."

"Not to us!" said Bradley.

"We didn't say hello to *you!*" said Lori. "Just him! Hello, Jeff."

"Hello," said Jeff.

Lori laughed.

"Why don't you just leave us alone, Bradley," said Melinda.

"No. You leave us alone first!" Bradley said, and he pushed Melinda.

She pushed him back. He pushed her again. She shoved him off the sidewalk.

He slipped on the wet grass and fell to the ground.

Lori laughed hysterically.

Bradley scrambled angrily to his feet. "You got my clothes dirty!"

"Bradley wet his pants!" teased Lori, hiding behind Melinda.

"Shut up!" he yelled.

"You started it," said Melinda.

"I'll punch your face in," said Bradley. He shook his fist at her.

Melinda raised her fists in the air.

He charged toward her, then kicked her in the leg.

She slugged him in the face with all her might.

Bradley stumbled backward and almost fell again, but caught his balance.

He glared at Melinda as his eyes swelled with tears. "No fair! Four against one!" he shouted, then ran home crying.

15.

"My poor baby," said Bradley's mother as she wrapped her massive arms around him.

He had stopped crying shortly after he ran away from Melinda, but started again when he saw his mother. "They beat me up and threw me in the mud," he sobbed.

His mother wiped his face with a tissue she kept rolled up in her shirt sleeve. "Come on," she said, and led him by the hand, down the hall to the bathroom. "You'll take a nice warm bath, put on clean clothes, and feel good as new."

Claudia was in the bathroom, combing her hair. "What happened to him?"

"Some bullies picked on him after school."

"There were four of them," said Bradley. "And they ripped up my homework too!"

"You've been crying!" Claudia accused.

"That's the rain," said Bradley.

Claudia started to say something but her mother told her to leave the bathroom. She laid out clean clothes on the bathroom counter, then started the water.

After his bath, Bradley went into his bedroom.

He was just in the nick of time!

Ronnie the Rabbit was romping across the bed,

singing "doo de-doo de-doo," when suddenly she was lost! "Where am I?" she asked.

Suddenly, three bad guys were chasing her. They were the Two of Spades, the Nine of Hearts, and the King of Diamonds. The King of Diamonds was the leader of the bad guys. "After her!" he yelled.

"Help!" called Ronnie. She ran to the edge of the bed—*the cliff!* She was trapped. The floor was a thousand feet below. The bad guys moved in for the kill. "Let me go!" she shouted, then fell off the bed onto the floor, but that was an accident. Bradley picked her up and put her back on the edge of the bed. It never happened. There was time out.

"What are you going to do to me?" asked Ronnie, trembling on the edge of the cliff.

"We are going to kill you," said the King of Diamonds.

"Oh no you're not!" said a voice from behind. It was Bartholomew.

"Get him, boys," ordered the King of Diamonds. The cards attacked.

Bartholomew punched the Two of Spades in the stomach, then flipped him over his head and over the cliff. "Aaaaaaaah . . ." the Two of Spades yelled as he fell a thousand feet to his death. Next, Bartholomew beat up the Nine of Hearts. "Go join your friend," he said as he threw him over the cliff too. "Aaaaaaaah," cried the Nine.

Now only the King of Diamonds was left. He came

at Bartholomew, swinging an axe. "I'll chop off your head!" he sneered.

Bartholomew ducked, then kicked the axe out of the King's hand and punched his face in. He threw the King over the cliff too.

Ronnie ran to Bartholomew. "You saved my life," she said.

"I know," said Bartholomew.

They kissed.

Claudia walked into the room. "Mom's making cookies because you got beat up," she said. "Ooh, you're going to have a black eye."

"I didn't get beat up," Bradley declared. "I beat them up. I gave one kid two black eyes, and another boy three."

"You can't give somebody three black eyes," said Claudia.

"Shut up!" said Bradley. "Or I'll give you four black eyes."

Claudia shrugged and left his room. Bradley got up from his bed and went into the kitchen, where his mother was making chocolate chip cookies. She let him lick the spoon.

"I want to know the names of the boys who did this to you," she said. "I'm going to call your school principal."

Bradley thought for a moment. "I don't know all their names," he said.

"Don't be afraid to tell me," said his mother. "They won't hurt you anymore."

Bradley thought a moment. "Jeff Fishkin!" he declared. "He was the leader of the gang."

"I'll call the school first thing in the morning," said his mother.

"Good!" said Bradley. "I hope he gets in trouble. I hate him."

16.

Bradley walked slowly, holding his hand over his eye so nobody would see it. His mother would have let him stay home from school, but his father said he had to go.

"He's scared," his mother had said. "Some bullies have been terrorizing him."

"Babying him will not solve the problem," said his father. "He has to learn to stand up for himself and fight back. The only reason the bullies pick on him is because they know he's afraid."

Bradley was afraid, but not of bullies. He wasn't scared of Melinda, either. It was little Lori Westin who scared him. He could picture her standing in the middle of the playground with her big mouth shouting for the whole school to hear: *"Melinda Birch beat up Bradley Chalkers and made him cry!"*

Cautiously, he walked across the schoolyard, hand over eye, and entered Mrs. Ebbel's class. He sat down in the last seat of the last row.

Jeff's chair was empty.

Good, he thought, still covering his eye. *He probably got kicked out of school.*

Out of his uncovered eye, he looked at the chart full of gold stars on the wall next to him. He was glad he didn't have any. He thought gold stars were ugly.

Mrs. Ebbel was in the middle of teaching the difference between adjectives and adverbs when she suddenly stopped and asked, "Bradley, is there something the matter with your eye?"

"No."

"Then please take your hand away from it."

"I can't," he said.

"Why can't you?"

He quickly tried to think of a reason why he had to keep his eye covered. His mind raced through a hundred ideas. "My hand's stuck," he said.

"It's stuck?" asked Mrs. Ebbel.

"I was gluing something and got glue on my hand, and then I accidentally touched my face with my hand and it got stuck."

"Bradley, take your hand away from your eye."

He grabbed his wrist with his free hand and pretended to try to pull it away. "I can't. It's stuck."

"Do you want to go to the principal's office?" she asked. "He's good at unsticking things."

"Wait, I think it's starting to loosen now," he said. He pried his hand away.

There was a bluish-black circle around his eye.

For a few seconds nobody said anything, then everybody started talking at once.

"What happened?" asked Mrs. Ebbel, but then quickly said, "Never mind, I don't want to know." She told the class to turn around, and started again on adverbs and adjectives.

Jeff walked in late. He said something to Mrs. Ebbel, then sat down next to Bradley.

Bradley looked the other way, at the chart full of

gold stars. Of all the stars, Jeff's were the ugliest.

For once, he wished he sat in the front of the room. Then only Mrs. Ebbel would have been able to see his face. Where he was, everyone could turn around and stare at him. All morning, Mrs. Ebbel had to keep telling kids to turn around and face front.

When the bell rang for recess, he put his hand over his eye and hurried outside. He went to the far end of the playground where nobody would bother him. But the word quickly spread that Bradley Chalkers had a black eye and kids kept wandering past him trying to get a peek.

"Melinda fights dirty," said Jeff, coming up behind him. "She hit you when you weren't looking. And you couldn't hit her back because it's impolite to hit a girl."

"Right!" said Bradley, turning around. "I would have punched her face in, except it's impolite. Melinda probably told the whole school that she beat me up, she's so stupid."

"No, I don't think she told anybody. After you left, she asked me not to tell anyone what happened. She made Lori and Colleen promise not to tell too."

"She's probably afraid I'll punch her face in," said Bradley.

"Probably," said Jeff. "Then, this morning I was called into the principal's office. He thought *I* was the one who hit you."

"Wha'd you tell him?" Bradley asked.

Jeff shrugged. "I told him you're my best friend."

"The principal's stupid," Bradley agreed.

64

17.

Jeff and Bradley ate lunch together around the side of the building, where nobody would bother them.

Jeff stood up. "I'll be right back," he said. "I have to go to the bathroom."

"Which one?" Bradley asked.

"Boys'," said Jeff.

"Oh," said Bradley "I'll wait for you here."

It was a very long wait.

"Hey, Jeff!" Robbie called as Jeff stepped out of the bathroom.

"Me?" asked Jeff. It surprised him because Robbie had always called him Fishnose or Fishbrain.

"Come over here," said Robbie. A group of boys was with him. Jeff recognized some from his class, but didn't know them all. One of the boys had a basketball.

"Hi, Jeff," said Brian, a boy from his class.

"Hi, Brian," he replied.

"How's it goin', Jeff?" asked Russell.

"Okay."

"This is Jeff Fishkin," Robbie told the boys who weren't in his class. "He's the guy who gave Chalkers the black eye."

"Way to go, Jeff!" said one of the boys he didn't know.

"All right, Jeff!" said another.

"Oh, man, would I have liked to have seen that."

"Man, when I saw Chalkers' eye today," said Robbie, "I just *smiled*. And then when I found out you got called to the principal's office, I thought, 'Way to go, Jeff.'"

"You didn't get in trouble, did you, Jeff?" asked Dan.

Jeff shook his head.

"They probably gave him a medal," said Russell, laughing.

The others laughed too.

"You like to play basketball, Jeff?" asked Andy, the boy with the basketball.

"Sure!" said Jeff.

They chose teams. Robbie and Andy were captains. Robbie had first pick. "I got Jeff," he said.

Jeff beamed.

They played basketball for the remainder of the lunch period. Jeff's team won, but it was also the team with five players. The other team had only four.

Everyone told him he played a great game.

"I always wondered why a guy like you was hanging around with Chalkers," said Robbie. "I guess it just took you a while to find out who your real friends were."

Jeff smiled. These were the kind of friends he had had back in his old school in Washington, D.C.

Of course, it meant he couldn't be friends with Bradley anymore, but . . . He shrugged.

18.

From around the corner of the brick building, Bradley watched the end of Jeff's basketball game. Every time Jeff took a shot, Bradley prayed he'd miss. When the bell rang, he hurried back to class ahead of Jeff and the other boys.

He sat at his desk—last seat, last row—and took out one of his books; it didn't matter which one. He stared at it very intently as Jeff sat down next to him.

Well, maybe it was okay for Jeff to have other friends, he decided as he turned a page. *I'm still his best friend. That's what he told the principal. Jeff wouldn't lie to the principal! Maybe I'll get to play basketball with his new friends, too, like Carla said.*

"Jeff," he whispered.

He wanted to tell Jeff that everything was still okay, that they could still be friends.

"Hey, Jeff!"

Jeff didn't look up from his work.

Jeff works hard, Bradley realized. *That's how he gets all the gold stars.*

He had to wait until after school.

"Hey, Jeff," he said as soon as the bell rang.

Jeff picked up his books and started out the door.

Bradley hurried after him. "Jeff!" he called. "Wait up."

Jeff stopped and slowly turned around.

Bradley suddenly felt very nervous. "Do you want to do our homework together?" he asked. "I can come over to your house if you want, or you can come over to mine. We can use my book. See." He showed Jeff his book.

"Hey, out of our way, Chalkers," said Robbie as he and Brian pushed past him.

"Chicken Chalkers," said Brian.

"Yeah, Chalkers," said Jeff.

Bradley walked away. He heard Jeff and his new friends laughing behind him.

But when he got home, his own friends were very glad to see him.

"We're so glad you're home," said Ronnie. "We missed you. We're glad you didn't go over to Jeff's house."

"You're our best friend," said Bartholomew.

"Hooray for Bradley!" shouted the wooden hippopotamus. "Hip . . . hip . . ."

"Hooray!" yelled all the other animals.

"Hip . . . hip . . ."

"Hooray!"

"Hip . . . hip . . ." said the hippo one last time.

"Hooray!"

"Let's play a game," said the donkey.

"What do you want to play?" asked Ronnie.

"Anything but basketball," said Bartholomew. "I hate basketball."

"Basketball is a stupid game," Ronnie agreed.

"It's the worst game in the world," said the hippopotamus.

"Why would anybody want to play *basketball?*" laughed the ivory donkey.

All the other animals laughed too.

19.

Everything returned to normal.

Bradley scribbled, cut up bits of paper, and taped things together. He hated everyone and everyone hated him. That was the way he liked it.

He shuddered whenever he remembered that he actually had almost done his *homework.* He couldn't imagine anything more horrible than that!

And he was glad Jeff wasn't his friend anymore. He realized he was better off without friends. In fact, he never was friends with Jeff! *I was just pretending to be his friend.*

He decided he'd never pretend to be anybody's friend again.

Jeff was normal now too. That was what he told Carla. He walked into her office and announced, "I don't need any help anymore. I have eight friends now. We play basketball every recess and lunch, and I'm the best player."

"Good for you, Jeff," said Carla. "I'm very proud of you."

"How many friends have you made?" he asked.

"I don't keep score," said Carla.

"I've made eight," said Jeff.

"I've always considered quality to be more important than quantity when it comes to friendship," said Carla.

"Eight," Jeff repeated. "And I'm not friends with Bradley anymore either."

"I'm sorry to hear that."

"Why? I'm not. I hate him. In fact"— he looked around the room—"I gave him a black eye!" He quickly glanced at Carla to see if she knew he was lying, then looked away.

"What happened?" Carla asked.

"Oh, you know, he wouldn't stop bothering me. I kept telling him to get lost, but he kept hanging around. I never liked him. No one does. Then he said to me, 'Give me a dollar or I'll spit on you!' Well, no one threatens me and gets away with it! I don't take that from nobody. So he tried to hit me, but I ducked, then punched his face in. I didn't want to do it, but I had no choice."

That was the short version. Jeff had told that same story to his eight new friends, but he usually made it much longer.

"So I don't think I need to see a counselor anymore," he said, "since I have eight friends."

"Okay, Jeff, if that's how you feel," said Carla.

"They might think I'm weird or something," he explained.

"Well, we can't have them thinking that."

"Does that mean I can go?"

Carla nodded. "But anytime you want to talk again, please feel free to come and see me." She smiled. "Even if you just feel like getting out of class for a while."

He left, glad to be out of there.

On his way back to class, he walked past the girls' bathroom. He stopped, shook his head, and chuckled to himself. It seemed like it was such a long time ago when he accidentally went in there. *I used to be such a jerk*, he thought.

He smiled a strange smile. He stretched his mouth so wide, it was hard to tell whether it was a smile or a frown.

20.

Colleen walked into Carla's office.

"I just came to tell you I can't talk to you," she said.

"Your parents didn't sign the form?"

"No, and they won't either! You know what they said? They said it was a waste of money for the school to hire you. They said you should get married and have your own children before you start telling other parents how they should raise theirs."

Carla shrugged.

"They said if I have any problems I should talk to them. But when I try to talk to them, they don't listen." She sighed. "Anyway, it doesn't matter. Jeff has lots of other friends now besides Bradley."

"Eight," said Carla with a smile.

"So now I can invite Jeff to my birthday party without having to invite Bradley. I can invite one of Jeff's other friends. Andy's nice. I couldn't invite Bradley even if I wanted to, because Melinda is my best friend, except for Lori, and she gave Bradley a black eye."

Colleen quickly covered her mouth with her hand, then slowly took it away. "That was supposed to be a secret," she said. "Melinda doesn't want anybody to know."

"I never repeat anything anyone tells me," Carla assured her.

"Good," said Colleen. "Melinda would kill me."

"Have you asked Jeff to your party yet?"

"No, not yet, but I will. I know he likes me because he always says hello to me when I say hello to him. But then I always get so scared. I never know what to say next. I wish you could help me. Why did my parents say such bad things about you? They don't even know you."

"Your parents are just trying to do what's best for you," said Carla. "A lot of people think counselors don't belong in schools." She shrugged. "I guess they're afraid I might fill your head with all kinds of crazy ideas."

21.

"Hello, Bradley," said Carla. "It's a pleasure to see you today. I appreciate your coming to see me." She held out her hand.

"I punched myself in the eye," he said as he walked past her. He didn't want her thinking someone else gave it to him. "I'm the only one who can beat me up."

"Did it hurt?" she asked.

"No," he said, sitting at the round table. "Nobody can hurt me. Not even me."

She sat across from him. She was wearing a light blue shirt with yellow mice running all over it. The shirt was the same color as her eyes. The mice were the same color as her hair.

"I wanted to hit somebody," he explained as he stared at her shirt. "But if I hit another kid, I would have gotten in trouble, so I hit myself."

"Why'd you want to hit somebody?"

"Because I hate him."

"Who?"

"Everybody."

"Is that why you hit yourself? Do you hate yourself?"

He didn't answer. He thought it was another one of her trick questions.

"Do you like yourself?" she asked.

He didn't trust that question either.

"Maybe the reason you say you don't like anybody else is because you really don't like yourself."

"I like myself," he said. "You're the one I don't like!"

"Tell me some things about yourself that you like."

He glared at her.

"I like you," she said. "I think you have lots of good qualities. But I want you to tell me things you like about yourself."

"I can't talk anymore," he said.

"Why not?"

"I'm sick. The doctor said I can't talk. The more I talk, the sicker I get."

"That sounds serious."

"It is! I've probably said too much already, and it's your fault. I'll probably throw up."

Carla nodded. "Don't say another word," she said quietly. "We'll just sit together in silence. Sometimes people can learn a lot about each other just by sitting together in silence." She locked her mouth shut, then opened it to swallow the key.

"You're weird," said Bradley.

"A lot of people tell me that," she admitted, then put her finger to her lips.

They sat together in silence. Bradley shifted in his chair. His eyes darted restlessly around the room. He put his hands behind his head and leaned back, then brought his hands out in front of him and folded them. Then he unfolded them.

He didn't like sitting together in silence. He thought she was probably learning too much about him. "I can probably talk a little bit," he said.

"No, I don't want you to get sick," said Carla. "I like you too much."

"The doctor says I'm supposed to talk a little, just not a lot."

"All right. Shall we talk about school?"

"No! The doctor says if I talk about school, I'll die!"

Carla frowned. "That's a problem," she said. "See, as part of my job, I'm supposed to help you do better in school. But how can I help you if we can't even talk about it?"

Bradley put his fingers to his chin and thought it over. "I know!" he said. "Just tell everybody that you tried to help me, but I wouldn't let you. Tell them that I was too mean and nasty. That's it. Tell them I said I'd spit on you."

"Oh no, I couldn't say that about you," said Carla. "You're too nice."

"They'll believe you," he assured her.

"It doesn't matter whether they believe me or not," said Carla. "I'd know it was a lie."

"So?"

"So when you tell a lie, the only person you're lying to is yourself."

He didn't see anything wrong with that. If you're only lying to yourself, and you know it's a lie, then it doesn't matter.

"I just wish I knew why a smart kid like you keeps failing."

"It's because Mrs. Ebbel doesn't like me," said Bradley.

"Shh!" said Carla. "Don't talk about it!"

"Well, I can probably talk about school a little bit without dying," he said.

"O-kay," Carla said hesitatingly, "but as soon as you feel even a little bit like dying, let me know and we'll stop."

They talked about school for about fifteen minutes before Bradley felt like dying. Carla pointed out that the same questions that were on the tests were also on his homework assignments. She suggested that if he did his homework, the tests might be easy for him.

"The tests *are* easy," he told her. "I could get a hundred if I wanted. I'm the oldest kid in the class. I answer all the questions wrong on purpose."

"You want to know what I think?" asked Carla. "I think you would like to get good grades. I think that the only reason you say you want to fail is because you're afraid to try. You're afraid that even if you try, you'll still fail."

"I'm not afraid of anything," said Bradley.

"I think you're afraid of yourself," said Carla. "But you shouldn't be. I have lots of confidence in you, Bradley. I know you'd do so well, if only you'd try. I can help you. We can help each other. We can try together."

It was then that he told her he couldn't talk about school anymore or else he'd die.

She thanked him for talking about it as much as he

had. "You were very brave," she said. She suggested that for their next meeting he make a list of topics to discuss so that they wouldn't have to risk talking about school again.

"Is that homework?" he asked.

"No-o-o," she assured him. "You don't even have to put your name at the top."

"Good," said Bradley. He was glad it wasn't homework.

It was time to return to class. "Thank you for sharing so much with me today," Carla said to him. "I enjoyed your visit very much." She held out her hand.

He stuck his hands in his pockets and walked out of her office.

22.

All week Bradley worked on his list of topics to discuss with Carla. *It's not homework,* he kept telling himself. *In fact, it's the opposite of homework! Because if I think of some good topics, then we won't have to talk about homework.*

He didn't scribble during class. He listened closely to what Mrs. Ebbel and the other kids said in order to get ideas for his list. He took it with him wherever he went. At recess, he kept his eyes and ears open, constantly on the lookout for a new topic.

The other kids were meaner to him than they'd ever been before. They were no longer afraid of him. They called him names, and when he didn't do anything about it, they called him more names.

A fourth-grade boy who wanted to show off to his friends ran up to him and said, "You're not even human! You're a monster! You're a monster from outer space!"

The boy ran away, but Bradley didn't chase him. He added three new topics to his list: Humans, Monsters, and Outer Space.

Monday was Halloween. Most of the kids brought costumes, which they were allowed to put on at lunch. Brian, one of Jeff's friends, didn't bring a costume. So he borrowed a black Magic Marker from Mrs. Ebbel and colored a circle around one eye.

When he came back from lunch, he told everyone he was a Bradley Chalkers.

While everyone laughed, Bradley busily worked on his list. It covered both sides of three sheets of paper.

1. Trees that lose their leaves
2. Gold stars
3. Chalk
4. Tape
5. Are chickens really afraid?
6. Why people laugh
7. What does it feel like to be shot in the leg?
8. Pencils
9. Pencil sharpeners
10. Accidents
11. Coffee
12. Military school
13. Canes
14. Basketball
15. Friends
16. Enemies
17. Hopscotch
18. Dodgeball
19. Four square
20. One potato
21. Two potato
22. Three potato
23. Four
24. Five potato
25. Six potato
26. Seven potato

27. More
28. Less
29. Nothing at all
30. What's it like to be in jail?
31. Good boys
32. Bad boys
33. Breakfast
34. Lunch
35. Dinner
36. Have you ever been to the White House?
37. Who shot my father?
38. Why did he get away?
39. Peanut butter and jelly
40. Gold stars
41. Black eyes
42. Fighting
43. Girls with big mouths!
44. What's it like inside a girls' bathroom?
45. Saying hello
46. Reflexes
47. Hate
48. When will I be able to grow a beard?
49. Things that smell bad
50. Things you like about yourself
51. Things you don't like about yourself
52. Things nobody likes about yourself
53. Things you don't like about anybody else
54. Gold stars
55. Does my head look like a chili bowl?
56. Closets
57. Hiding places

58. Dreaming
59. Bad dreams
60. I wish I could fly.
61. Kids with glasses
62. Glasses you drink from
63. Why people like some people and hate other people
64. Breaking things
65. I wish I was invisible.
66. Cry babies
67. What happens to you when you grow old?
68. Humans
69. Monsters
70. Outer space
71. Why is Halloween a holiday?
72. Pirates
73. Princesses
74. Ghosts
75. What happens when you die?
76. What if you were never born?
77. Can someone else be you?
78. Can you be someone else?
79. If I was someone else, I wouldn't make fun of me.
80. Magic
81. Markers

He didn't go trick-or-treating that evening, though Ronnie and Bartholomew did. The other animals gave them lots of candy.

"I'm making a list of topics to talk about with

my counselor," he told them. "Do you have any ideas?"

"How about rabbits?" suggested Ronnie.

"That's a good one," said Bradley. He added "Rabbits" to his list.

"Bears," said Bartholomew.

"That's good too."

Claudia barged into his room.

Bradley quickly shoved his list under the pillow on his bed.

"How about what Dad's going to do to you when he finds out you're flunking?" she asked. "That's a good topic."

"What are you talking about?" asked Bradley.

"The list."

"What list?"

"Oh, I don't know," said Claudia. She slowly wandered toward the bed, then lunged for the pillow.

Bradley dived for it, too, but Claudia beat him to it. She held the list above her head and read it. As she looked at each new page, she cracked up laughing.

"What's so funny?" he demanded.

"Your list!"

"What's wrong with it?"

"This isn't the kind of stuff you talk about with a counselor."

"How do you know?"

"Chalk?" asked Claudia. "What can you say about chalk?"

"A lot!" he insisted.

Claudia laughed. "One potato! Two potato! Your counselor's going to be mad when she sees this."

"Give it to me!"

"Yes," she answered as if he had asked a question.

"Yes, what?"

"Yes. Your head looks like a chili bowl." She laughed.

"Shut up!"

" 'Who shot my father?' " read Claudia. "How's she going to know that?"

Bradley shrugged.

Claudia gave him back the list. "You wrote 'Gold stars' three times," she said, shaking her head.

Bradley grabbed it from her hand and looked at what he'd written.

"That's the stupidest list I've ever seen," said Claudia. "Your counselor's not going to want to talk about anything on that list."

"You don't know her," he replied. "She'll talk about anything I want to talk about. She listens to me. She likes me!"

"No she doesn't," scoffed Claudia. "That's just her job!" She walked out of his room, laughing.

Bradley watched her go. Then he added two new topics to his list: Sisters and Jobs.

Tears filled his eyes as he tried to think of another topic. He crossed off two of the "Gold stars," then crumpled the list into a ball and threw it in his trash basket.

23

"Look out! Here comes the monster!" screamed a chubby fourth-grade boy. "It's the monster from outer space!"

"Aaaah! It's so ugly!" yelled his skinny friend.

"Don't let it touch you!" warned a girl with pink glasses. "Or you'll turn into a monster too."

Bradley ran at them. They scattered and regrouped, like pigeons.

He sat down to eat his lunch.

"It sure is a stupid monster!" shouted a third-grader.

After lunch, Bradley sat at his desk—last seat, last row. He didn't look at Jeff. He didn't look the other way, either, at the chart full of gold stars. And he didn't look straight ahead, at Mrs. Ebbel. He didn't look anywhere.

It was time to see Carla again. He took the hall pass from Mrs. Ebbel and walked out of the classroom.

He hated Carla. He didn't want to make the same mistake with her that he had made with Jeff. He realized Claudia was right. Carla didn't like him. That was just her job.

She was waiting for him outside her door. "Hello, Bradley," she said as she held out her hand. "It's a pleasure to see you today. I appreciate your coming to see me."

He walked past her and sat down at the round table.

She sat across from him. She was wearing a long-sleeved white shirt with two triangles on it, one red and one blue.

"Did you make a list of topics to discuss?" she asked.

"No, you're the teacher."

"So?"

"So you're the one who has to say what we talk about, not me. That's your *job!*"

"Well, let me think," said Carla. "Are you sure you can't think of anything?"

He shook his head.

"I'm surprised. I thought you would have come up with a lot of interesting topics. Well, in that case, we'll have to talk about school. Shall we start with homework?"

"Monsters from outer space," he replied.

"Hmm?"

"Monsters from outer space," he repeated. "You said I could pick the topic. I want to talk about monsters from outer space!"

"What a wonderful topic!" said Carla.

"The only way to kill them is with a ray gun," said Bradley. "Regular guns, or even hand grenades and atomic bombs, won't kill them. You need a ray gun." He stood up and pretended to shoot a ray gun, making a noise that sounded like a cross between a machine gun and a horse.

Carla put her hands up to protect herself. "Don't shoot me," she said.

"You're a monster from outer space," he told her.

"No I'm not. I'm a counselor."

He stopped firing. "Do you believe in monsters from outer space?"

She shook her head. "No. But I do believe there are other types of creatures living in outer space. I just don't believe in monsters. I believe that Earth is just one small planet in a gigantic universe. I think there are billions of other planets with trillions of other kinds of creatures living on them. Some are real stupid and others smarter than you or me. Some are bigger than dinosaurs; others, smaller than ants. But out of all those creatures, I don't think there is even one monster."

"Not even one?"

"No," said Carla. "I think everyone has 'good' inside him. Everyone can feel happiness, and sadness and loneliness. But sometimes people think someone's a monster. But that's only because they can't see the 'good' that's there inside him. And then a terrible thing happens."

"They kill him?"

"No, even worse. They call him a monster, and other people start calling him a monster, and everyone treats him like a monster, and then after a while, he starts believing it himself. He thinks he's a monster too. So he acts like one. But he still isn't a monster. He still has lots of good, buried deep inside him."

"But what if he's real ugly?" asked Bradley. "What if he has green skin, and only one eye in the middle of his face, and three arms, and two hands on each arm, and eight fingers on each hand?"

Carla laughed. "You and I might think that's ugly," she said, "but that's just because it's different from what we're used to seeing. On that planet, that might be considered beautiful. You may have just described a handsome movie star."

Bradley laughed.

"On that planet, they probably would think I was ugly, because I don't have green skin and I have two eyes."

Bradley shook his head. "No, they might think I was ugly, but not *you*."

"Why, Bradley," Carla said with astonishment, "that's the nicest thing you've ever said to me. Thank you."

He blushed. He hadn't meant it the way it came out. "I don't want to talk about monsters anymore," he mumbled.

"Okay," said Carla. "I think we had a very good conversation, don't you? You picked an excellent topic."

For the rest of the session, he colored. He took a green crayon out of Carla's large box of crayons and tried to draw the creature from outer space that he had described. He was able to draw the three arms, and six hands, but he had trouble fitting eight fingers onto each hand.

He looked up. "Carla?"

"Yes, Bradley."

"Can you see inside monsters?" he asked. "Can you see the 'good'?"

"That's all I see."

He returned to his picture. He drew a black eye in the middle of the creature's face. He drew a red heart inside the creature's chest to show all the "good" that was there.

"Well, how does a monster stop being a monster?" he asked. "I mean, if everyone sees only a monster, and they keep treating him like a monster, how does he stop being a monster?"

"It isn't easy," Carla said. "I think, first, he has to realize for himself that he isn't a monster. That, I think, is the first step. Until he knows he isn't a monster, how is anybody else supposed to know?"

Bradley finished coloring and showed his picture to Carla. "He's a movie star on his planet," he said. "Everyone loves him."

"He's very handsome," said Carla.

"You want it?" asked Bradley. "I mean, I don't want it anyway, so you can have it."

"I'd love it!" said Carla. "Thank you. In fact, I'm going to hang it on the wall right now."

Bradley watched her tack it up. He almost told her she wasn't allowed to put holes in the wall, but he changed his mind.

It was time for him to go back to class.

"I'm looking forward to seeing you next week," said Carla. "I hope you have another wonderful topic for us to discuss."

He started to go, then stopped and turned around.

"Yes?" she asked.

He put his hands on his hips and stared at her.

"Did you forget something?"

He stood and waited.

Her eyes suddenly lit up. She held out her hand and said, "I enjoyed your visit very much. Thank you for sharing so much with me."

He stretched his mouth into a half smile/half frown, then hurried out of her office.

24.

"Here he comes," said Lori. "Don't be a chicken."

Colleen bit her bottom lip.

It was after school. The three girls stood across the street and watched Jeff.

"Maybe we should wait until tomorrow," said Colleen.

"Hey, Jeff!" Lori shouted.

"No," Colleen whispered.

Jeff turned.

Lori and Melinda walked toward him. Colleen lagged behind.

"Hello, Jeff," said Lori.

"Hi, Jeff," said Melinda.

"Hello, hi," answered Jeff.

Lori laughed.

"C'mon, Colleen," said Melinda. "Ask him."

Colleen blushed and looked away.

"Colleen has something she wants to ask you," said Lori.

"Well, see, um, okay, well—" stammered Colleen.

"Quit bothering me," Jeff said very quietly.

"We're not *bothering* you," said Lori. "Colleen just wants to ask you—"

Melinda stopped her. "Let Colleen ask him," she said.

"Well, see," said Colleen. "Okay." She took a breath. "I'm having a . . . it's my birth—"

"I don't want her asking me anything!" Jeff snapped.

Colleen turned bright red.

"And quit saying hello to me too!"

"We can say hello if we want," said Melinda. "It's a free country."

"I don't want you saying it to me," said Jeff.

"Don't worry!" Colleen exploded. "I won't!"

"I will," said Lori. "Hello, hello, hello, hello, hello."

"Shut up!" said Jeff. He slammed his book down on the sidewalk.

"Hello, Jeff, hello, Jeff," said Lori. "Jello, Jeff." She laughed at her mistake. "Jello, Jeff. Hello, Jello." She laughed hysterically.

"And quit laughing!" Jeff shouted.

"She can laugh," said Colleen. "You can't tell her she can't laugh."

"Hellohellohellohellohellohello," said Lori as fast as she could.

"Shut up!" screamed Jeff.

"You shut up," said Melinda.

"I'm not afraid of you, Melinda," said Jeff.

"I'm not afraid of you either," said Melinda.

Jeff raised his fists in the air. Melinda did the same. Lori shrieked with anticipation.

"Okay, hit me," said Jeff.

"You hit me first," said Melinda.

"No, you hit me first," said Jeff.

"Somebody hit somebody!" shouted Lori.

Jeff tapped Melinda's shoulder with his fist.

She slugged him in the stomach. As he bent over she hit him in the nose. Jeff flailed his arms as he tried to defend himself, but Melinda kept punching him, in the neck, in the stomach, then in the eye.

Jeff fell to the ground.

Melinda jumped on top of him, knees first. She sat on his chest and held his arms flat against the ground.

Lori knelt beside them and slapped the ground as she counted: "One . . . two . . . three . . . four . . . five . . . six . . . seven . . . eight . . . nine *ten!*"

Melinda stood up.

Lori held Melinda's arm high in the air. Holding her nose with her other hand, she bellowed: "The winner, and still champion of the world . . . Marvelous Melinda!"

Colleen clapped her hands.

25.

I'm going to be good, thought Bradley, *and then, when everybody sees how good I am, they'll know I'm not a monster.*

"And Mrs. Ebbel will give you a gold star," said Ronnie.

Bradley was so excited, he didn't realize he was putting on two different-colored socks: a blue one and a green one. He tied his shoelaces, then went into the bathroom and looked at himself in the mirror.

His black eye was almost all gone. It had faded into a light brownish-yellowish color. He hurried out to breakfast.

His mother made oatmeal for him.

"I hate hot cereal," he complained.

"You'll eat what you're served," said his father. "This isn't a restaurant."

He frowned, not because he had to eat oatmeal, but because he realized he never should have said he hated it. That was something the Bad Bradley would say. The Good Bradley liked hot, lumpy cereal.

He took a big spoonful, brought it to his mouth, and swallowed the glop. "Mmm, good!" he said, but as he withdrew the spoon from his mouth, his elbow bumped his glass of orange juice.

Claudia screamed and jumped up.

"Oh, Bradley!" said his mother.

His father glared at him.

"It was an acci—" He started to say it was an accident but then remembered Carla didn't believe in accidents. That puzzled him. He wondered why he would want to spill his orange juice on purpose. He liked orange juice. It was the oatmeal he should have spilled.

"Are you just going to sit there, or are you going to help your mother clean it up?" asked his father.

He picked up his napkin to help, but his mother told him to stay out of her way. "You'll only make a bigger mess," she said.

Silently, he finished eating.

As he headed back to his room, Claudia burst out laughing.

"What's so funny?" he demanded.

"Look at your socks!" she laughed.

He looked down at his feet, then back at his sister, the laughing hyena. "Thank you, Claudia," he said. "I appreciate your sharing that with me."

She stopped laughing and stared at him.

He walked into his room, sat on the edge of his bed, and took off his sneakers.

"Wow!" said Bartholomew. "You were so good. I would have punched her face in if I was you."

"He's going to get a gold star today," said Ronnie.

Bradley changed his socks, but once again he was so excited thinking about the gold star that he didn't pay attention to what he was doing. He took the green sock off his right foot. He took the blue sock off his left foot. He put the green sock on his left foot and the blue sock on his right foot. Then he put his shoes on and left for school, determined to be good.

He walked into class and took his seat—last seat, last row. He sat up straight with his hands folded on top of his desk. He tried to hold back his excitement as he glanced at the chart on the wall next to him.

Jeff came in and sat down—last seat, second to last row.

Bradley saw him out of the corner of his eye, then turned to get a better look. Jeff had a black eye!

"What are you staring at, Chalkers!" Jeff snarled.

"Hey, you two look like twins!" exclaimed Shawne, the girl who sat in front of Jeff.

"Turn your ugly face around," Jeff snapped.

"Oh, shut up, Bradley," said Shawne, turning around.

Bradley looked at the back of Shawne's head. *She still thinks I'm a monster,* he realized. *But once I get my gold star, then she'll know I'm good.* For the rest of the morning, he sat at attention with his eyes fixed on Mrs. Ebbel. He kept wondering if she had noticed how good he was yet.

As he walked outside for recess, he was almost certain there'd be a gold star next to his name when he returned.

Curtis and Doug, two of Jeff's friends, came out of Mrs. Sharp's class. "What's the big idea?" asked Doug.

"Hitting Jeff when he's not looking," said Curtis.

"Huh?" said Bradley.

Doug pushed him.

He stumbled backward into Jeff, who pushed him back the other way.

Bradley looked around. He was surrounded.

"Jeff's our friend," said Robbie.

"Yeah!" said Brian.

"You hit me when I wasn't looking!" said Jeff. "And my hands were full of groceries. I didn't want to break the eggs."

"Chicken Chalkers," said Dan.

There was a space between Andy and Doug. Bradley dashed through it and ran across the playground.

Jeff and his friends chased after him.

Bradley looked back at them and smashed into a girl standing on one foot. The girl fell onto the hard hopscotch ground and wailed.

"I'm telling, Bradley!" said one of her friends.

"I'm sorry," Bradley said helplessly, then continued running. He ran up the concrete steps and entered the school building through the auditorium. From there, he walked quickly to the library.

"What do you want, Bradley?" asked Mrs. Wilcott, the librarian.

"Nothing," he muttered as he sat down at one of the tables. He leaned his head against his hands, propped up by his elbows.

What if Carla's wrong? he worried. *What if I really am a monster?*

"I don't want any trouble from you, Bradley," said Mrs. Wilcott.

26.

"We'll get you at lunch, Chalkers," Robbie whispered as Bradley returned to class.

"You're late," said Mrs. Ebbel.

He sat at his desk—last seat, last row—and looked at the chart on the wall next to him. Of course there was no gold star next to his name. He had already done three things wrong: First, he had knocked over a girl and made her cry. Second, he was late getting back to class. And third and worst of all, his name was Bradley Chalkers. As long as his name was Bradley Chalkers, he'd never get a gold star. They don't give gold stars to monsters.

They beat up monsters. He looked around at Jeff, Robbie, Russell, and Brian. He had to concentrate very hard to keep from crying.

The worst part wasn't getting beaten up. The worst part was that he knew everyone would love it so much. He imagined the whole school—the boys, the girls, and even the teachers—standing by and cheering as Jeff's gang took turns hitting and kicking him.

When the bell rang for lunch, he slowly took his paper sack out of his desk.

"We'll be waiting for you outside," Jeff said to him.

Bradley watched him walk out the door. He walked

slowly toward the front of the room, then suddenly dashed out the other door and into the hall.

"Bradley! Come back here!" Mrs. Ebbel yelled.

He kept running. So what if he got in trouble? What difference did it make?

He pulled on the door to the library. It wouldn't budge. The library was closed during lunch.

He tried to think of somewhere else he'd be safe.

"There he is!" said Doug, stepping out of the auditorium.

Bradley turned and ran back the way he had come. He rounded a corner, then stopped and made a quick and desperate decision.

He opened the door to the girls' bathroom, closed his eyes, and stepped inside.

He opened his eyes. Luckily, the room was empty.

He held his breath and listened. Nothing could be worse than being beaten up inside a girls' bathroom. *They'd probably stick my head in a girls' toilet*, he thought.

He waited. He didn't hear anything.

He looked around. The floor and the bottom half of the walls were covered with green tile. There were two white sinks and a paper towel dispenser. There were three toilets in three separate stalls. Each stall had a door. It looked very much like the boys' bathroom. Girl toilets appeared to be the same as boy toilets. He was disappointed.

He couldn't risk going back out into the hall. He leaned against one of the stalls, reached into his

100

brown paper sack, and took out his roast beef sandwich.

Someone was opening the door! He quickly put the sandwich back in the bag and hopped into a stall, closing the door behind him. He stood on the toilet so his feet couldn't be seen.

He listened.

He heard a person walk across the tiled floor and then enter the stall next to him. He covered his mouth with his hand as he heard some familiar but very private sounds.

At last the toilet flushed and he heard the person zip her pants and walk across to the sink. He heard the sound of running water, and then a paper towel pulled down from the dispenser. Finally, the bathroom door opened and shut.

He exhaled, hopped off the toilet, stepped out of the stall, and froze.

Two girls were staring at him. One was the girl who had used the toilet next to him. The other had just entered. He wondered which was which. Then he heard the loudest scream he'd ever heard in his whole life. That answered his question.

He darted past them, opened the door, and flew into the hall.

He rounded a corner, came to a door, and pounded wildly on it until it opened.

"Bradley?" said Carla.

"Hello, Carla." He held out his hand. "It's a pleasure to see you today."

27.

She shook his hand.

He walked inside, shut the door behind him, and sat down around the table. "You won't believe it," he said as he looked at his picture of the green monster hanging on the wall. "You just won't believe it."

"I'm sure I won't," Carla agreed. She sat across from him. She was wearing a sleeveless, black-and-white checkered shirt.

"Okay, I'll tell you," said Bradley.

"I was hoping you would."

"Do you know where I was before I was here?"

"No?"

He slammed his fist on the table. "The girls' bathroom!"

He told her all about it, how the girl had used the toilet next to him and how he thought she had left but really another girl had entered! "At first I didn't know which girl was which, but then one of them screamed, so she must have been the one."

"Who was she?" asked Carla. "Did you know her?"

"Yes, but I don't think I should tell you her name. She probably doesn't want anybody else to know."

"That's very considerate of you, Bradley."

He shrugged.

"Shall we have lunch?" asked Carla.

"Okay." He took out his roast beef sandwich.

Carla set her lunch on the table. She had a carton of yogurt and a plate of sliced tomatoes and cucumbers.

"That looks good," said Bradley.

"You want to trade?"

"Okay."

They traded lunches. Bradley ate a slice of cucumber. He thought it was delicious.

"So what were you doing inside the girls' bathroom?" asked Carla. She took a big bite out of Bradley's roast beef sandwich.

"Jeff and his friends were chasing me," he explained. "Jeff's got a black eye, just like me! They all think I gave it to him."

"Did you?"

He could have lied. He could have said, sure, he beat up Jeff with one hand tied behind his back. He knew Carla always believed whatever he said.

"No. I can't even beat up a girl," he said. "Melinda Birch beat me up. Do you know her?"

"No."

"You'd like her. She's nice."

Carla smiled.

Bradley ate a slice of tomato followed by a spoonful of yogurt. "I hid in the library at recess," he said. "They couldn't beat me up in the library, even if they found me. You can't even *talk* in the library."

"Yes, I know."

"Isn't it amazing?"

"What's that?"

"The library. All those books. And they're all different, aren't they?"

Carla nodded as she drank Bradley's juice through a straw.

"I kept thinking about that the whole time I was there," he said. "They're all different, but they all use practically the same words. They just put them in a different order."

"Did you—?"

"Just twenty-six letters," he told her. "All they do is move those letters around and then they say so many different things!"

"Did you—?"

"You'd think, after a while, they'd run out of ways to move them around," said Bradley.

"Did you check out a book?"

"No, Mrs. Wilcott won't let me. I used to, a long time ago, before I met you, I used to check out books and not return them. I used to scribble in them and rip them up. So she won't let me check any books out anymore. The whole time I was there she kept watching me, saying, 'I don't want any trouble from you, Bradley.' "

He ate another slice of cucumber. "I just wanted to look at a book. I wasn't going to ruin it."

"I know," said Carla. "And after a while, Mrs. Wilcott will know that too."

"I'm trying to be good," said Bradley. "But nobody will give me a chance."

"They will. It just takes time."

"Do you ever play checkers on your shirt?" he asked.

Carla nearly spit out her juice. She laughed and shook her head.

"I like your shirts," he said.

"I like your socks," said Carla.

Bradley looked at his mismatched socks. "I thought I changed them," he said, befuddled.

"I hate socks that match," said Carla. "See." She stuck out her legs. She was wearing white pants. She had on one white sock and one black sock.

Bradley smiled. It wasn't his usual twisted smile, but one that was genuine. It was one that, up till now, had been seen only by Ronnie and Bartholomew.

"I know something good you can do," said Carla. "And Mrs. Ebbel will notice it too."

"What?"

"Homework."

The smile dropped off his face. "No. No I can't," he said.

"Sure you can," said Carla.

"I can't!" His eyes filled with tears.

"You can do anything you want to do, Bradley Chalkers. I have a lot of confidence in you."

He shook his head. "But I can't." His voice cracked.

"Don't say 'I can't.' As long as you say you can't do something, then of course you won't do it. Say, 'I can!' Say 'I can!' and you can do anything."

"I can't! I can't!" He was crying.

"Bradley, it's not that difficult. You're making a big

deal out of nothing. If you want, I will help you."

"I can't," he sobbed.

"Why can't you?" she demanded.

He wiped his eyes with his sleeve and sniffled. He looked Carla straight in the eye and said, "I don't know what page we're on!"

"Oh, Bradley," Carla whispered. Her eyes glistened. She stood up, walked around the table, and kissed him on the cheek.

28.

Bradley lay on his bed, on his stomach. He chewed the end of his pencil as he looked hopelessly at the arithmetic book, opened in front of him.

Next to the book was a piece of paper. In the upper right-hand corner he had written:

> Bradley Chalkers
> Homework
> Arithmetic
> Page 43
> Red Hill School
> Room 12
> Mrs. Ebbel's class
> Last seat, last row
> Black eye

His handwriting, which was messy anyhow, was made worse by the fact that he wrote with a dull pencil on top of a soft bed.

He had stayed in Mrs. Ebbel's class as long as he could after the bell rang.

"Bradley, it's time to go home," Mrs. Ebbel finally said to him.

He looked outside, unsure if Jeff and his gang of bullies were waiting for him. "Um, I have a question," he said.

Mrs. Ebbel eyed him suspiciously. "What kind of question?"

He tried to figure out what kind of question he had. "An *asking* question."

"I see," said Mrs. Ebbel.

"May I ask it?" he asked.

"O-kay," she said reluctantly.

He asked his question. "What page is the homework on?"

"The homework? Page forty-three."

He wrote "43" on the top of his sneaker so he wouldn't forget, then took his arithmetic book and stepped outside. Jeff and his friends were playing basketball. He ran home.

Now he looked hopelessly at page 43, shook his head, and sighed.

Question 1. What is three-fourths of two-thirds?

It was the most impossible question he'd ever seen. His mind wandered.

"Hey, Bradley, what are you doing?" asked Ronnie.

"Homework."

"What's homework?" she asked.

"It's work you do at home."

"Is that supposed to be funny?" she asked.

"No, really. That's what they do at school. They give you work to do at home and they call it homework."

"You've never done it before," said Ronnie.

"I'm doing it for Carla. Now leave me alone so I can concentrate."

Question 1. What is three-fourths of two-thirds?

"Why are you doing it for Carla?" Ronnie asked.

He sighed. "Okay, I'll tell you, but you can't tell anyone."

Ronnie promised not to tell.

"We're in love."

"Really?" exclaimed Ronnie. "How do you know?"

"She kissed me."

"Oooh, that means she loves you!" said Ronnie. "Are you going to marry her?"

"Maybe, when I'm older. First, I have to do my homework."

"I'm going to marry Bartholomew," said Ronnie.

"I know," said Bradley. "Now let me do my homework."

Question 1. What is three-fourths of two-thirds?

"Hey, Bradley, what's going on?" asked Bartholomew.

"Leave him alone," said Ronnie. "He's trying to do his homework. He can't concentrate when you're talking to him."

"Maybe I can help," said Bartholomew. "What's the problem?"

"What is three-fourths of two-thirds?" Bradley asked.

"Three-fourths of two-thirds," Bartholomew repeated. "That's a tough problem all right. Three-fourths of two-thirds. Let's see. You divide four into—no, you multiply two times, no . . ."

"*Of* means *divide*," said the donkey. "Like if you

take half of something it means you divide by two. You divide three by two and four by three."

Bradley started to write that down.

"No, *of* means *times*," said the lion. "You have to multiply everything."

"First you have to reverse the nominators," said the fox.

"You don't reverse, you inverse," corrected the mother cocker spaniel.

"I think you have to find a common denumerator," said the elephant.

"Not for multiplication," said the hippopotamus. "That's only for addition."

"Multiplication is the same as addition," said the fox, "only faster."

"You cancel out the threes," said the kangaroo. "You always cancel out threes."

"You multiply the threes," said the lion.

Bradley kept erasing and rewriting and erasing and rewriting until there was nothing but a big black smudge covering his paper. On top of the smudge, he tried to write $3 \times 3 = 9$, but as he did so, his pencil tore a hole through the paper.

"The answer can't be nine," said Ronnie. "If you start out with fractions, you have to end up with fractions."

Bradley slammed the book shut. "None of you know what you're talking about!" he cried out in disgust. He took the book, paper, and pencil, and walked down the hall to the dining room.

His mother was sitting at the table working a cross-word puzzle from the newspaper. He plopped down next to her and sighed.

She looked at him inquisitively.

"I can't figure out how to do my homework," he complained. "Will you help me?"

His mother smiled. "I'd be delighted. Let me see."

He pushed his arithmetic book in front of her. "Page forty-three."

She opened the book to that page and looked at Bradley's torn, smudged paper. "Okay. First let me clear away this newspaper so we can have a nice, neat place to work. While I do that, I want you to get a clean sheet of paper."

"I don't have any more paper. This is all I brought home."

"There's some paper in your father's desk. Get a sharp pencil, too."

He looked at her in disbelief. He wasn't allowed to touch anything on his father's desk.

She nodded.

Bradley felt a little scared as he walked into the extra bedroom which his father used as an office. He opened the top drawer of the old oak desk and carefully took out a pencil and a piece of paper. He shut the drawer, looked around, then hurried back to his mother.

She smiled at him.

He sat down and wrote, much neater this time:

Bradley Chalkers
Homework
Arithmetic
Page 43
Red Hill School
Room 12
Mrs. Ebbel's class
Last seat, last row
Black eye

"You have to put all that," he explained, "in case it gets lost."

She read the first question aloud. " 'What is three-fourths of two-thirds?' "

He shrugged.

"Okay," she said, "the first thing you want to do is write the equation."

He still didn't know what to do.

She wrote it for him.

$$\frac{3}{4} \times \frac{2}{3} = \underline{\hspace{2cm}}$$

"Whenever you see the word *of*, it means you multiply," she explained.

"*Of* means *times*," he said.

"Right," said his mother.

That was what the lion had said.

"Now you can cancel out the threes," said his mother.

That was what the kangaroo had said. You always cancel out threes.

112

Neither of them noticed that Claudia was standing behind them, watching. "That's not how you're supposed to learn it," she said abruptly.

Bradley turned around and glared at her.

"You have to explain *why* you cancel them," said Claudia. "And they don't call it canceling. It's called dividing by one."

"I just know the way I learned it," said Mrs. Chalkers.

"If you want, I can show you, Bradley," said Claudia.

He looked at his mother, then back at Claudia, then at his mother.

"She knows the way they're teaching it now," said his mother.

"You'll help me?" Bradley asked his sister.

"Sure, why not? I got nothing better to do."

Mrs. Chalkers stood up, and Claudia took her place. "Don't do it for him," said Bradley's mother. "Make sure he knows how to do it himself."

Claudia worked patiently with Bradley for the rest of the afternoon. When he said he understood something, she made him explain it to her. That was harder. He understood it when she did it, but then he had trouble when he tried to do it himself.

By dinnertime, they were only a little more than halfway through. Bradley wanted Claudia to help him after dinner, too, but she had her own homework to do.

"You know how to do it," she told him. "You can do it yourself."

"I need help," he complained.

"I'll help you," said his father.

"You will?"

"Let's go to my office. We can work at my desk."

Bradley couldn't believe it.

They worked together. Bradley was surprised by how much his father knew. He made all the hard parts seem easy. Bradley was a little disappointed by how quickly they finished. He had liked working with his father.

He brought his finished homework back to his room.

"Oh, I get it, Bradley," said Bartholomew. "You multiply the numerators and denominators separately. But I still don't understand reducing."

"It's easy," said Bradley. "Here, let me show you again."

29

Bradley was too excited to sleep. *Mrs. Ebbel will be so surprised,* he thought. *She'll tell the whole class, "Only one person got a hundred percent—Bradley!"*

But there were so many things that could still go wrong. *What if I lose it on the way to school?* he worried. *What if Jeff and his friends steal it?* Twice during the night he got out of bed to make sure it was safely folded inside his arithmetic book.

What if I did the wrong page? He was no longer sure whether Mrs. Ebbel had said page 43 or page 62! He tried to remember exactly what she said to him.

He sat up in horror. She never said it was *arithmetic* homework. Mrs. Ebbel had just said a page number. She never said what book! She could have meant history, or language, or any of his other books!

He lay back down and trembled. His tears wet his pillow.

He got out of bed early in the morning, checked to see if his homework was still there, then quickly got ready and left for school without eating breakfast.

On the way he stopped to make sure he still had his homework. As he opened his book, the paper fell onto the sidewalk, right next to a puddle of water.

He stared at it, horrified by what he had almost done, then quickly picked it up and placed it back in his book. He held the book tightly shut the rest of the way to school.

He was one of the first ones there. He had to wait for the doors to open. He kept on the lookout for Jeff and his gang. He stood with his back to the school wall so they couldn't sneak up behind him.

He saw Andy. He thought Andy had seen him, too, but if he had, he didn't do anything about it.

When the doors opened, he was the first one in Mrs. Ebbel's class. He sat at his desk—last seat, last row—and waited.

As the other kids came in, he saw them put sheets of paper on Mrs. Ebbel's desk. He wondered if that was their homework. He now had a new worry. He didn't know how he was supposed to turn in his homework.

Jeff entered, placed a piece of paper on the pile on top of Mrs. Ebbel's desk, then came toward the back of the room.

It must *be his homework*, thought Bradley. *What else could it be?*

"Shawne," he said aloud.

The girl who sat in front of Jeff turned around.

"Are you supposed to put your homework on Mrs. Ebbel's desk?"

"Don't tell me what to do, Bradley!" Shawne snapped. "You worry about your homework, and I'll worry about mine, okay?" She turned back around.

It was almost time for school to start. *What if I have to put it on her desk before the bell rings or it doesn't count?* He fumbled through his book for his homework, stood up, then headed for Mrs. Ebbel's desk.

He became more nervous with each step he took. His mouth was dry and he had trouble breathing. He could hardly see where he was going. He felt like he was going to faint. Mrs. Ebbel's desk seemed so far away. It was like he was looking at it through the wrong end of a telescope. His heart pounded and his homework rattled in his hand.

Somehow he made it to her desk and tried to focus on the sheets of paper the other kids had put there. It looked like arithmetic homework! Page 43!

But instead of feeling better, he felt worse—like he was going to explode.

"Do you want something, Bradley?" asked Mrs. Ebbel.

He looked at his homework shaking in his hand. Then he tore it in half and dropped it in the wastepaper basket next to Mrs. Ebbel's desk.

He instantly felt better. His head cleared and his breathing returned to normal. His heart stopped pounding.

He walked back to his desk, took a deep breath, exhaled, and sat down. He folded his arms on his desktop and lay his head down sideways across them. He felt sad, but relieved, as he gazed at the gold stars.

30.

Bradley remained in his seat after everyone else had gone out to recess. He walked to Mrs. Ebbel's desk.

She was sorting papers.

"Mrs. Ebbel," he said timidly. "May I use the hall pass? I have to see the counselor."

She looked up.

"Please."

Normally Mrs. Ebbel would never allow Bradley Chalkers loose in the halls, but something about the way he asked must have changed her mind. "All right, Bradley," she said, then caught herself. "But if you're bad, you'll never be allowed in the halls of this school again!"

"Thank you."

He took the hall pass off the hook behind her desk and headed out the door.

"You're welcome," Mrs. Ebbel said to herself.

He knocked on the door to Carla's office.

"How nice to see you today, Bradley," she greeted him. "I appreciate your coming to see me."

He shook her hand, then they sat around the round table. She was wearing the shirt with the squiggles on it. It was the one she wore the first time he saw her. He liked it, but not as much as the one with the mice.

"I did my homework last night," he said.

Carla beamed. "I'm so proud of—"

"I ripped it up."

"What?"

"I ripped it up. I brought it to school, and I was just about to put it on Mrs. Ebbel's desk, but then I ripped it up."

"Why did—?" Carla started to ask.

"Why did I rip it up?" he asked her first.

"I don't know, why did you?"

He shrugged.

She shrugged.

They both giggled.

"I was afraid you'd be mad," Bradley said when he stopped giggling.

Carla shook her head. "You did your homework, that's the important thing. I'm so very proud of you, Bradley Chalkers."

"I'm going to do all my homework, from now on," he promised.

"That's wonderful!"

"But what if I keep ripping it up?" he asked.

"Why would you want to do that?"

"I don't know. I didn't think I wanted to rip it up, today."

"The main thing is that you did it. And you learned some things by doing it, didn't you?"

"What 'of' means," said Bradley.

"What 'of' means?" Carla repeated.

"Times," said Bradley.

She stared at him, baffled. "Oh, right!" she said, as it all suddenly connected for her. "Okay, so even though you ripped up your homework, you still remember what you learned. You didn't rip up your memory. And when Mrs. Ebbel gives the next arithmetic test, you'll know how to answer the questions."

"If they don't change the rules," said Bradley.

"What rules?"

"Like, what if they decide to make *of* mean subtraction?"

"They won't change the rules," Carla assured him, "whoever *they* are."

"But what if I rip up my test, too?" he asked.

Carla looked at him as if he was being silly. "Has Mrs. Ebbel given you any homework for tomorrow?" she asked.

"Tomorrow's Saturday."

"Okay, for Monday?"

"No, we never have homework over the weekend." He spoke like an expert, like he'd been doing homework for years. "But we have a book report due next week. Only . . ."

"Only what?"

"I don't have a book. And Mrs. Wilcott won't let me check out any from the library."

"Well, let's see," said Carla. "Do you think you might know somebody else who might let you borrow a book? Think hard now."

Bradley looked around at all the books in her office. "May I borrow one of yours?" he asked. "Please. I won't scribble in it."

Carla walked around the table, then picked out a book from a stack on top of one of her bookcases. "It's my favorite," she said as she gave it to Bradley.

He read the title and laughed. *My Parents Didn't Steal an Elephant,* by Uriah C. Lasso.

He opened to page one and read the first sentence.

I hate tomato juice.

He thought that was a funny sentence to start a book. He continued reading.

Every morning, Aunt Ruth gives me a glass of tomato juice, and every morning I tell her I hate it. "Fine, Dumpling," she always says, "don't drink it."

She calls me Dumpling. Uncle Boris calls me Corn Flake. They're crazy. One of these days I'm afraid they're going to try to eat me.

He glanced up at Carla, then returned to the book.

My parents are in jail. They got arrested for stealing an elephant from the circus. Only they didn't do it. If they stole an elephant I'd know about it, wouldn't I? I mean, if your parents stole an elephant, don't you think you'd know about it?

I think the elephant just ran away. Her master was always mean to her. He whipped her and made her do stupid tricks. My parents used to complain about that a lot. That's why everybody thinks they stole her.

So, anyway, that's why I have to live with my crazy Aunt Ruth and Uncle Boris. If you ask me, they belong in the circus. They're crazy!

Uncle Boris always smokes a cigar. It just hangs out of the corner of his mouth. Whenever he kisses my aunt, he swings the cigar out of the way with his tongue, and kisses her out of the side of his mouth.

I bet you think Aunt Ruth doesn't like it when he kisses her that way. Wrong. She always laughs when he does it. Sometimes she smokes a cigar, too. I told you they were crazy.

Look! He even smokes his cigar while he's drinking tomato juice.

The bell rang. Bradley was amazed by how quickly the time had passed. "Do you want to have lunch together again?" he asked.

"I'm sorry. I'm having lunch with the president of the school board," said Carla. "I'd much rather eat lunch with you."

He didn't mind too much. At least he had her book to read.

They shook hands, then he walked back to class. He placed the hall pass back on the hook and took his seat.

He knew he'd write a good book report because he had such a good book to read. *I just hope I don't rip it up.*

31.

"Whatcha doin', Bradley?" asked Ronnie.

"He's *reading*," Bartholomew replied nastily. "He says he doesn't want to be *disturbed*. He thinks he's too good for us now that he does his homework."

"Oh, be quiet and let him read if that's what he wants to do," said Ronnie.

"Thanks, Ronnie," said Bradley. "I knew you'd understand."

"*I knew you'd understand*," mimicked Bartholomew.

Ronnie understood. She knew about Carla.

Bradley returned to his book.

Uncle Boris and Aunt Ruth are married. I bet you thought you already knew that, except you're not as smart as you think you are. They were my uncle and aunt even before they got married. Uncle Boris is my mother's brother and Aunt Ruth is my father's sister. They didn't even know each other until my parents got arrested for stealing the elephant. Then they both came here to *take care of me*. Hah! They fell in love and got married a week later. It was sickening! You're lucky you weren't here.

I've been cheated out of an aunt and an uncle. If they had each married somebody else, then I'd have two aunts and two uncles. Now I only have one aunt and one uncle. I wonder what happened to the aunt and uncle I don't have. I wonder if they married each other, too.

Bradley looked up. He tried to make sense out of that last paragraph. It made him think. A lot of parts in the book made him think. That was one of the things he liked about it. It made him think about his father, too. About why the man who shot him wasn't in jail.

There was a knock on the door. His mother entered holding a piece of paper. "Oh, you're reading," she said. "That's good."

"It's a good book," he replied.

"I just got this letter from the Concerned Parents Organization," she said. "There's going to be some sort of meeting about Miss Davis, your counselor."

Bradley's heart fluttered.

"It says if I have any complaints I should come to the meeting." She shrugged her shoulders. "I don't think I have any complaints. She seems to be helping you. Do you have any complaints?"

"Oh, no! He doesn't have any complaints." Claudia laughed, coming in behind her mother. "He's in *love* with her. I heard him say it to his animals."

"What?" Bradley exclaimed in a very high voice.

Claudia snickered. "Look, Mom, he's blushing! That proves he loves her."

Bradley wished he could crawl under his bed and hide.

"It doesn't prove anything," said Mrs. Chalkers. "Quit teasing your brother."

"Where'd you get the book, Bradley?" Claudia asked, like she already knew the answer.

His heart was beating very fast. "Carla gave it to me."

"*Carla* gave it to him," Claudia repeated.

"Well, I don't care where he got the book," said Mrs. Chalkers. "I'm just happy to see he's reading it."

"The only reason he's reading is because he's in love with his teacher," said Claudia.

"She's not my teacher, she's my counselor," said Bradley.

Claudia roared with laughter. His mother laughed, too, but she quickly covered her mouth.

"I didn't say I was in love with her!" Bradley insisted. "We were just talking about my counselor, not my teacher, that's all!"

"Are you going to let him marry her, Mom?" asked Claudia.

Mrs. Chalkers smiled. "Well, I don't know. She seems like a very lovely girl."

Bradley felt like he was going to die. His sister was hysterical.

"So you don't have any complaints about Miss Davis?" his mother asked seriously, getting back to the letter.

"She's okay," he said without emotion.

Claudia snickered.

"Well, then, I won't go to the meeting," said his

mother. "C'mon, let's leave your brother alone."

"The Concerned Parents Organization never likes anything," said Claudia. "They're always causing trouble at my school, too. They want to turn kids into robots."

Bradley watched his sister and mother walk out of his room and shut the door behind them.

He lay down on his bed. His face was on fire. "So, I love her? What's wrong with that?"

"Nothing," said Ronnie. "They just don't understand about love."

The door opened again. Claudia stuck her face inside and said, "If the Concerned Parents Organization ever found out Carla kissed you, she'd be fired for sure!"

32.

Bradley paid close attention as Mrs. Ebbel taught arithmetic. He nodded his head every time she said something that he already knew. Once he almost raised his hand to answer a question, but he lost his nerve. Somebody else gave the answer he would have given. *I knew it*, he thought as he nodded his head.

He had spent recess in the library reading *My Parents Didn't Steal an Elephant* by Uriah C. Lasso. When he was leaving the library, Mrs. Wilcott stopped him and said, "You were reading, weren't you?"

"Yes."

"Good for you, Bradley! Good for you!"

He smiled now as he remembered it. *It's because of Carla's book*, he thought. The book was his lucky charm. As long as he had it with him, it seemed like nothing could go wrong.

His black eye was all gone too.

When the bell rang for lunch, he put his arithmetic book away, took out his lucky book, and walked to Mrs. Ebbel's desk. "May I please borrow the hall pass?" he asked.

She let him have it. He knew she would. He was holding the magic book.

He walked to Carla's office. Just as he was raising his fist to knock, she opened the door. "Bradley, what a pleasant surprise!"

"You want to have lunch together?" he asked.

"Oh, I'm sorry, I can't. I have to go to the principal's office."

"What's the matter? Did you get in trouble?" he joked.

She didn't laugh at his joke. She shrugged her shoulders, then headed toward the principal's office.

Maybe she really did get in trouble, Bradley thought as he watched her go. *It's probably because she doesn't believe in rules. She must have broken one without knowing it. I should have warned her.* But he wasn't too worried. He couldn't imagine anything bad ever happening to Carla.

He walked through the auditorium and outside to the playground. He sat down on the steps outside the auditorium and ate his lunch. At least he had her book with him. That was almost as good as eating lunch with her.

He didn't read while he ate. He was afraid he might accidentally spill food on the book even if there were no such things as accidents.

Colleen Verigold walked by.

"Hello, Colleen!" he called to her.

She stopped and looked at him oddly, then walked away without returning his hello.

Bradley didn't mind. He had said hello to Colleen because he knew Carla would appreciate it. He felt

Carla was watching over him. And it didn't matter that Colleen didn't say hello back, because in his heart he heard Carla say, *Hello, Bradley. It's a pleasure to see you today.*

He finished eating, then opened the book.

Guess what they've done now? They wallpapered the garage. I told you they were crazy! Whoever heard of anybody putting wallpaper on the walls of a garage? Purple paper with yellow polka dots!

I don't even know how they got in there. The garage has been locked shut for months. The lock was broken or something so nobody could get in.

At least I'm glad they finally got it open. It was beginning to smell pretty bad. You could smell it from the driveway. Now it just smells like paste.

I can't wait until my parents get home and put an end to all this craziness. Their trial is next week. They have to be found innocent.

I mean, if they stole an elephant I'd know about it, wouldn't I? Where could you hide an elephant?

"Look, he's reading," said Robbie.

"I didn't know he knew how to read," laughed Curtis.

Bradley looked up. He was surrounded by Jeff and his gang.

"He can't read," said Brian. "He just looks at the pictures!"

They all laughed.

"Whatcha readin'?" asked Russell.

Bradley closed the book and slowly stood on the concrete steps.

"Chicken Chalkers," said Dan.

Andy bounced a basketball.

Bradley glanced behind him. Doug was blocking the door to the auditorium. "What's the matter, Brad-ley?" he asked.

"Hey, Chalkers, what's the name of your book?" asked Robbie.

He looked at his book, then stared defiantly at Robbie.

"Let me see it," said Robbie.

Bradley clutched it against his chest. No matter what, he wasn't going to let them harm Carla's book.

"Aw, c'mon, Bradley, be a pal," said Robbie. "I just want to see it."

Curtis chuckled.

Robbie stepped up toward him. "You can't read anyway," he said. "Give it to me and I'll read it to you." He reached out and rested his hand on the book.

Bradley jerked it away.

"Uh-oh, I think he's getting angry," said Brian.

"I just want to see it," said Robbie. Again, he reached for the book.

Bradley held it under his left arm and against his chest. He made his right hand into a fist.

Robbie backed away. "Jeff," he called.

"C'mon, Jeff, teach him a lesson," said Dan.

Jeff stepped between Andy and Russell.

"All right!" said Curtis.

"Hold on," said Andy. "Let'm get off the steps."

The boys backed up. Bradley, clutching his book, walked down the concrete steps to where Jeff was waiting.

"Do you want me to hold your book, Bradley?" said Andy.

Bradley glanced at him.

"Don't worry," he said sincerely. "I won't hurt it."

Bradley handed Andy the book, then looked back at Jeff.

They stood on a patch of grass and dirt and faced each other. The bruise around Jeff's eye had turned brown with a greenish tint. Jeff raised his fists.

The other boys formed a circle around them.

"C'mon, get'm, Jeff," urged Brian.

"Give him another black eye," said Russell.

Bradley readied himself. He raised his fists in the air, then lowered them. He had an idea.

"Hello, Jeff," he said.

Robbie snickered.

Jeff stared at him, wide-eyed. "Hello, Bradley," he replied.

Bradley smiled. He held out his hand.

Jeff smiled too. It was his first honest smile in a long time. He shook his best friend's hand.

The other boys were dumbfounded. No one said a word.

Andy finally broke the ice. "Do you like to play basketball, Bradley?" he asked.

Bradley looked at him, bewildered. "I'm not very good," he said.

"So? None of us are," said Jeff, patting him on the back.

"Now we'll have even teams!" said Robbie.

33.

Bradley was *terrible!*

He dribbled with two hands. He passed the ball to people who weren't on his team. But, worst of all, whenever anyone passed the ball to him, he said "thank you."

He never shot at the basket. He didn't dare. Finally, after his team was losing 28 to 6 anyway, everyone told him to try a shot.

He looked around for someone to pass to.

Jeff sat down so Bradley wouldn't pass it to him. "Just shoot," he said.

The rest of his team sat down too. "Shoot it!" they said.

Everybody on the other team sat down too. "Shoot the ball!"

Bradley faced the basket. His tongue slipped out the corner of his mouth as he carefully aimed, then threw the ball high in the air. It hit the back of the rim, bounced against the backboard, then dropped through the net.

"Great shot!" said Jeff.

"Way to go," said Andy, patting him on the back.

At first he couldn't believe it, but then he saw Carla's book, lying on the ground at the base of the basket. *No wonder,* he realized.

Everyone headed for the water fountain. Bradley went along, too, even though he wasn't thirsty. But then, once he got there, he realized he was thirsty. He just hadn't noticed.

"Good game, Bradley," said Brian.

"You just have to stop passing to people who aren't on your team!" said Dan.

"Maybe you should give the rest of us on your team black eyes too," said Robbie. "Then you'll know who to pass to."

Everyone laughed, even Bradley.

He and Jeff were the last two left at the water fountain. Everyone else had already started back to class. As they drank, their eyes met and they broke up laughing.

"How *did* you get the black eye?" Bradley asked after he stopped laughing.

"Melinda," said Jeff.

Bradley nodded. "She's strong," he said.

"Oh boy, you can say that again," said Jeff.

They laughed again.

"My book!" Bradley suddenly exclaimed. He ran back to the basketball court where he'd left it.

Jeff shook his head as he watched Bradley run away. *Life's weird,* he thought.

He walked into the boys' bathroom and splashed his sweaty face with cold water. He had to hold the faucet down with one hand and splash his face with the other.

Colleen Verigold walked in.

He stared at her.

She looked around, then screamed and ran outside.

Jeff watched the door swing shut behind her.

34.

Life was too weird for Jeff to return to class.

Anytime you want to talk again, Carla had said, *please feel free to come and see me. Even if you just feel like getting out of class for a while.*

He hoped she had really meant it. He had a lot he wanted to say to her, beginning with "I'm sorry."

He slowly walked to her office. He hoped she wasn't with somebody else. He knocked.

Carla opened the door and smiled when she saw him. "Hello, Jeff."

He smiled. "Hi, Carla. I'm—"

He stopped because he saw somebody else sitting at the round table.

"I believe you two know each other," said Carla.

Jeff lowered his eyes. "Hello, Colleen," he muttered.

Colleen Verigold covered her face with her hands.

"You don't mind if Jeff joins us, do you, Colleen?" Carla asked.

Colleen shook her head with her hands still over her face.

Jeff awkwardly sat down. "Mrs. Ebbel doesn't know I'm here," he said.

"I'll write you a note," said Carla.

Colleen peeked out from between her fingers. "I'm not supposed to be here either," she said.

Carla turned to Colleen. "So what's the big emergency? Can you say it in front of Jeff?"

"He already knows," said Colleen. She looked at Jeff. "You better not tell anybody!"

"I won't," Jeff promised.

"Tell anybody what?" asked Carla.

"Colleen walked into the boys' bathroom," said Jeff. "I was there washing my face."

"Jeff!" Colleen exploded. "You just promised you wouldn't tell!"

"Oops," said Jeff. He blushed. "It was only Carla. You were going to tell her anyway, weren't you?"

Colleen smiled at him. "I didn't go there on purpose," she explained to Carla. "It was an accident."

"I don't believe in accidents," said Carla.

Colleen stared at her in amazement. She wondered how Carla knew she had gone in after Jeff on purpose. She turned to Jeff. "I'm sorry for saying hello to you when you didn't like it."

"That's okay."

"Anyway, how was I supposed to know you didn't like it? You always said hello back."

"I know. I can't help it. Whenever anybody says hello to me, I always have to say hello back." He looked at the picture of the green monster with six hands hanging on the wall. "If a big scary monster said, 'Hello, Jeff,' I'd probably say hello back to it, too."

Colleen laughed.

"Well, what's wrong with that?" demanded Carla. "If a monster says hello to you, you should say hello to it. If you don't, then I have to wonder which one of you is really the monster."

Colleen frowned. She suddenly remembered that Bradley Chalkers had said hello to her at the beginning of the lunch period and she had walked away without saying hello back. It made her feel terrible.

"You can say hello to me whenever you want," said Jeff.

She smiled again. "Hello, Jeff," she said.

"Hello, Colleen," said Jeff.

"I read somewhere," said Carla, "that in Zen, the most important rule is that when one person says hello to you, you have to say hello back."

"What's Zen?" asked Colleen.

"A religion," answered Carla. She got a book from her bookcase. "Here it is." She read aloud from *Raise High the Roof Beam, Carpenters* by J.D. Salinger: " 'In certain Zen monasteries, it's a cardinal rule . . . that when one monk calls out "Hi" to another monk, the latter must call back "Hi!" without thinking.' "

"Jeff should be a Zen monk!" Colleen exclaimed with delight.

Jeff laughed. "I already say hello to anybody who says hello to me," he said proudly.

"Can girls be Zen monks too?" Colleen asked.

"Why not?" asked Carla.

Colleen laughed with delight. Then she said, "Jeff, do you want to come to my birthday party next Sunday?"

"Yes!" said Jeff. "That's the second most important

rule about being a Zen monk. Whenever another Zen monk invites you to a birthday party, you have to say yes!"

Colleen laughed again. "You're the only boy so far," she said. "I'll invite one more, but only one. I can't invite too many boys."

Suddenly she looked very serious. She knew what she had to do.

35.

Before dinner, while it was still light, Bradley's father, bad leg and all, taught Bradley how to dribble. Bradley could hardly wait to show his friends.

The next morning, when the bell rang for recess, everyone hurried outside.

Except Bradley.

First, he had to put his paper *neatly* in his notebook. Then he had to mark his place in his book and put all his pencils in his pencil holder. Then he put everything away, *neatly*, in his desk.

He rushed out the door.

"Hello, Bradley," said Colleen.

He stopped cold.

Colleen closed her eyes tightly, then opened them. With the determination of a Zen monk, she asked, "Would you like to come to my birthday party on Sunday?"

Bradley stared at her.

"Jeff will be there," said Colleen. "He's the only other boy. Everyone else will be girls. I would have invited you sooner, except, um, I just found out when it was."

Bradley nodded his head until his mouth worked. "Yes!" he said.

"Good," said Colleen, then scooted away.

Bradley stared after her, then turned around in a

circle as he tried to remember which way he was going.

"Bradley!" called Andy. "Hurry up! We need you."

He ran to the basketball court. He forgot everything he had learned about dribbling.

"Is he coming?" asked Melinda.

Colleen nodded.

Lori stuck out her tongue and screamed.

"It'll be fun," said Melinda. "Bradley's not the same as he was. I think he's gotten better."

"Oh, you can't come anymore, Melinda," said Colleen.

"Why not?" she asked, obviously very hurt.

"Because they're coming, and you beat them up!"

"But they started it."

Colleen stared at her, hands on hips. She couldn't believe Melinda was being so unreasonable.

"I thought I was your best friend," said Melinda.

"You are," said Colleen. "But they're *boys*. Oh, okay. You can come. But you better not cause any more trouble."

"I thought *I* was your best friend," said Lori.

That night Bradley lay in bed, too excited to sleep. He couldn't wait until tomorrow when he'd see Carla again. He had so much to share with her. And it was all because of her magic book.

He turned on the light above his head and read aloud to Ronnie and Bartholomew. They laughed whenever he did.

"I just met Ace. He's my parents' lawyer. Guess what? He's crazier than my Aunt and Uncle put together.

The first thing he said to me was, 'Do you like peanuts?'

'They're okay,' I answered.

'Good,' he said. He gave me a peanut and I ate it.

'Do you want another peanut?' he asked.

I shrugged.

So he gave me another peanut and I ate that one, too. Big deal.

'You must really like peanuts a lot,' he said.

I told you he was crazy.

'I want you to remember that,' he said. 'If anybody asks you, you really like peanuts a lot.'

'Okay, I really like peanuts a lot,' I said.

Then he gave me three more peanuts! 'Eat these!'

I ate them.

'You just ate three peanuts in five seconds,' he said. Can you believe it? He had timed me. Tell me he isn't crazy!"

"He isn't crazy," laughed Ronnie.

"Why is he making such a big deal over peanuts?" asked Bartholomew.

"I don't know," said Bradley.

There was a loud knock on his door, then his father entered. "It's past your bedtime, Bradley," he said.

"Okay," said Bradley. He reached for his light.

"Oh, you were reading," his father noticed. "Well, that's all right then. You can stay up if you want to read."

Bradley smiled. Once again, the magic book had kept him from getting into trouble.

"So, what did the kids think of your dribbling?"

"I forgot how," Bradley admitted. He hated to disappoint his father.

"I guess we need to practice more," said his father. "Maybe this weekend I'll put up a backboard on the garage." He said good night and walked out of Bradley's room.

"Come on, I want to hear about the peanuts," said Bartholomew.

Bradley continued reading.

"So then he asked me, 'Are you good at math?'

Well, I don't like to brag but math happens to be my best subject. Big deal.

'Okay, here's a math problem for you,' he said. 'If you can eat three peanuts in five seconds, how long would it take for you to eat fifty thousand peanuts?'

I got out a pencil and paper and figured it out. 'About twenty-three hours and nine minutes.'

'That's less than a day, isn't it?' he asked.

'Yes,' I said. 'There are twenty-four hours in a day.' He's supposed to be my parents' lawyer and he doesn't even know how many hours there are in a day!

'Remember that,' he told me. 'If anybody asks you, you can eat fifty thousand peanuts per day.'

I laughed. 'Who would ask me that?'

'The police.' "

The chapter ended there.

36.

Bradley giggled as he walked to Carla's office for his regularly scheduled appointment. He couldn't wait to tell her all that had happened to him. *She'll be so happy!* he thought.

She was waiting for him in the hall, just outside her office. But before she could say anything, he beat her to it. "Hello, Carla," he said. "It's a pleasure to see you today. I appreciate coming to see you."

She smiled. "The pleasure is mine," she replied.

He laughed. He got a kick out of being polite.

They shook hands, then went inside to the round table. She was wearing a dark blue shirt, almost black, with little white stars on it. She looked like nighttime.

"So what's new?" she asked.

He opened his mouth, but nothing came out. He didn't know why, but for some reason he didn't want to tell her. "What's new with you?" he asked.

"With me?" asked Carla. "Nobody's ever asked me that before."

"You're always asking me what's new," he said. "Why can't I ask you?"

"You can!" she replied. "You can ask me anything you want. Let me see. What's new? I bought a new shower curtain yesterday. But that doesn't sound like very interesting news, does it?"

"What color?"

144

"Oh, sort of beige, I don't know, it doesn't really have a color."

"That's a good color," said Bradley. "It sounds beautiful."

"It's okay," said Carla.

"What happened to your old shower curtain?" he asked.

"It started getting a little rotten," said Carla.

"Was it also beige?"

"Um, no," said Carla. "I think it was yellow when it was new, but it was sort of a greenish brown when—"

"Colleen invited me to her birthday party!" he blurted. Then it all came pouring out of him.

"Jeff's invited too. We'll be the only boys. Everyone else will be girls. Jeff and I are friends now. The other guys like me too. We play basketball together. At first I was afraid to shoot the ball, but then everybody said, 'Shoot, Bradley, shoot,' so I shot and made it! Everyone was amazed. So was I. I still miss a lot more than I make, but I'm getting better. Everyone says so. My father taught me how to dribble. He's going to put a basket over the garage. At first they wanted to beat me up, but I said, 'Hello, Jeff,' and he said, 'Hello, Bradley,' and then Andy asked me if I wanted to play basketball. Then Colleen asked me to her birthday party and I said, 'Yes,' and she said, 'Good.' She would have asked me sooner except she just found out when she was born."

Fortunately, Carla had heard most of it already, otherwise she wouldn't have understood a thing he said.

"It's all because of you," said Bradley.

"You did it, Bradley, not me."

"It was your magic book!"

"My book? What's that got to do with— Bradley, what's wrong?"

He was crying. One second he was beaming about her magic book, and the next he was sobbing and shaking all over.

"Bradley?"

He covered his face with his hands. Tears spilled out of his eyes.

"What is it?" asked Carla. "What happened?"

He shook his head.

Carla rose from the table, got a box of tissues, and placed it in front of him.

He pulled out a tissue, but didn't use it. "I've never been to a birthday party," he blubbered. Then he hiccupped. "Not a real one, where other kids are there." He hiccupped again, then blew his nose. "A long time ago, when I was in the third grade I went to one, but then they made me go home because I sat on the cake."

"Well, you're a lot smarter now than you were when you were in the third grade," said Carla.

"But I don't remember what to do!" Bradley whined. "Do I have to bring my own chair?"

"Why would you have to bring your own chair?"

"For musical chairs. That's why I sat on the cake. I got mad because there was no place else to sit." He sniffled. "Will there be ice cream?"

"Don't you like ice cream?"

"What if they don't have enough for me? What if they only have enough for everybody else? And what about pin the tail on the donkey?"

"You don't have to bring your own donkey," said Carla.

He laughed through his tears. "But what if I stick it in a bad place?"

"You want to know what I think?" asked Carla. "I think you're a little overwhelmed by all that has happened to you. It's scared you. You think you're Cinderella."

"Cinderella?" he repeated, and laughed again.

"You're Cinderella and you've just been invited to the ball and now you're afraid that right in the middle of Colleen's birthday party, everything will suddenly turn into a pumpkin!"

He wiped his eyes on his tissue.

"You're afraid all the good things that happened will suddenly disappear. You're afraid everyone will suddenly stop liking you. But this isn't a fairy tale, Bradley. Your friends like you for who you are. My book wasn't magic. The magic is in you."

"Do I have to bring her a present?" he asked.

"You don't *have* to do anything," said Carla. "But it's a nice thing to do, don't you think? Colleen invited you to her birthday party because she likes you, and you give her a present because you like her and because you want to help celebrate her birthday."

"What should I get her? Should I get her a doll? Is that what girls like?"

"I don't know. Everyone likes different things. Give

her something you like. If you like it, then she probably will too. Give her a gift from the heart."

"How about a shower curtain?" he asked.

"If it comes from the heart," said Carla.

He smiled.

When it was time for him to return to class, Carla said, "I enjoyed our visit very much. Thank you for sharing so much with me."

"The pleasure was mine," he replied. He had been waiting to say that.

37.

The meeting between Carla Davis and the Concerned Parents Organization was held after school in room 8, a second-grade classroom.

Carla sat in a chair that was too small for her and faced the parents. She crossed her ankles and folded her hands on her lap. The five members of the school board sat behind her. The principal sat next to her, at the teacher's desk.

Bradley's mother wasn't there. She was out with Bradley, shopping for Colleen's birthday present. Since she didn't have any complaints, she didn't come to the meeting. The only parents who came were those who had complaints.

"I'd like to know what we need a counselor for?" asked a father. "Kids have enough *counseling*. What they need is more discipline. If they're bad, they should be punished!"

The other parents clapped their hands.

"We need to get *back to basics*!" said a woman. "Reading, writing, and arithmetic. And, of course, computers."

Her husband had a chart that showed that if the counselor was fired, there would be enough money to put a computer in every classroom.

Everyone got very excited about that idea. They all loved computers.

"No one is being fired," said the principal. "The purpose of this meeting is to give you a chance to ask Miss Davis questions."

"She told my son it was good to fail!" shouted a woman standing under a poster of an octopus. "She told him grades didn't matter."

"I never said it was good to fail," Carla calmly replied. "I simply tried to help him relax. Children learn better when they're not under pressure. They do better when they can enjoy school."

"My son doesn't go to school to *have a good time*," said the woman. "He has to get good grades so he can get into a good college!"

The principal reminded the parents that Miss Davis wouldn't see any of their children without their permission.

"But why should our tax dollars pay for her to counsel other people's children?" one of the mothers complained.

Several other parents agreed.

A woman with red hair stood up. "My daughter came home with one of those forms for us to sign, and we refused to sign it. We didn't want her seeing the counselor. We try to give her all the counseling she needs at home. But then we found out the counselor's been talking to her anyway."

"What's your daughter's name?" asked the principal.

"Colleen Verigold."

Carla admitted that she had seen Colleen without

her parents' permission. "Colleen came into my office very upset and said she had to talk to me. She said it was an emergency."

"What kind of emergency?" asked the school board president.

"It was something very personal," said Carla.

"But what was it?" asked the school board president.

"I'm sorry," said Carla. "I never repeat anything a child tells me." She knew Colleen wouldn't want everybody to know she had gone into the boys' bathroom.

"You're not supposed to see a child without her parents' permission," said the school board president. "Now if it was an emergency, then you might have been justified. But we have to know the nature of the emergency."

"I'm sorry," said Carla.

"You can tell me," said Mrs. Verigold. "I'm her mother. If there was an emergency, don't you think I should know about it?"

"Ask Colleen. If she wants to tell you, she will. I can't break my promise to her."

"But Colleen's just a child," said a member of the school board. "You don't have to keep promises to children."

"I do," said Carla.

"She's been trying to make her change religions," said Colleen's mother. "Colleen came home from school and announced she didn't want to be Catholic anymore. She wants to be a Zen monk!"

Carla laughed, though she knew that was a mistake. She tried to explain about saying hello back to someone who says hello to you, but nobody seemed to understand what that had to do with being a Zen monk.

"You're not allowed to teach religion in public school," said the president of the school board. "And you weren't even supposed to talk to her child in the first place." He apologized to Colleen's mother and assured her it wouldn't happen again.

A woman in the front row raised her hand. "I never had a counselor when I went to school," she said. "I don't understand what they do, exactly."

"Why don't you explain to the parents what you do and how you help different children?" the principal suggested.

"Mostly, I just talk with them," said Carla. "I listen to their problems, but I never tell them what to do. I try to help them to learn to think for themselves."

"But isn't that what school is for?" asked the woman. "To tell kids what to think?"

"I believe it's more important to teach them *how* to think, instead of *what* to think," said Carla.

"But if they do something bad, don't you tell them it's wrong?" asked the man sitting next to her.

"No," said Carla. "I think it's much better if they figure that out for themselves."

"What if there was a boy who bit his teacher?" asked a father.

152

"What?" Carla exclaimed.

"Wouldn't you tell him not to bite her?" he asked.

"No, I'd talk to him about it and try to find out why he bit her, but—"

"What if he keeps on biting her?" asked the man. "What if every day he sneaks up behind her and bites her on her butt? Then what would you do?"

"This is getting ridiculous," said Carla.

"Tell him what you'd do," said the principal.

Carla sighed. "I'd try to help the boy understand the reason he wants to bite his teacher, and then help him reach the conclusion that he shouldn't do it."

"How long would that take?" asked a woman.

"I don't know."

"A month?"

"Possibly."

"And meanwhile he keeps biting his teacher!" said the first man. "She could get seriously hurt!"

"She could die," said another man. "How would you feel then?"

"What if the kid had rabies?" someone else shouted. "Don't you think he should get a rabies shot?"

"I bet you'd feel differently if he bit you on your butt!" someone called from the back of the room.

Everyone began talking at once.

"What if he bit you?"

"You'd punish him then, wouldn't you?"

"Then you wouldn't wait for him to think for himself, would you? Not if he bit you!"

"What if he bit you?"

Carla uncrossed her ankles, then crossed them the other way. As she looked at the angry group of parents, she had the horrible feeling that they all wanted to bite her butt.

38.

Bradley Chalkers
Homework
Book Report
My Parents Didn't
Steal an Elephant
By Uriah C. Lasso
Mrs. Ebbel's class
Room 12
Red Hill School
Last seat, last row
Next to Jeff

<u>My Parents Didn't Steal an Elephant</u>
by
Uriah C. Lasso
by
Bradley Chalkers

<u>My Parents Didn't Steal an Elephant</u> was a
very funny and crazy book by Uriah C. Lasso, a
funny author to write such a book. It is a story
told by a kid. The kid's parents are in jail because
they stole an elephant, except they are innocent.
Hey! I just realized something. You know what?
You never know the kid's name! I just realized

that. You know what else too? You don't know if the kid is a boy or a girl! I just realized that right now as I was writing this book report because I didn't know whether to write he or she. I told you it was crazy!

The kid lives with his aunt and uncle. They're crazy too. They put wallpaper up in the garage for no reason. I told you they were crazy.

Ace is crazy too. He's the lawyer for the kid's parents. He makes the kid practice crying for an hour every day so the kid will be able to cry good in court. Only when the kid finally gets to court, the kid doesn't cry. The kid laughs!

Then everybody else laughs too. Then the kid's parents get to go home because they're innocent.

Except, do you want to know something? I'm not so sure! I mean, if they really were really innocent, then who ate all the peanuts?

I told you it was crazy. The end.

The End

"Absolutely wonderful!" said Carla.

"Is it good?" asked Bradley.

"You captured the very essence of the book."

He smiled even though he didn't know what *essence* meant.

They were sitting around the round table. It was Thursday before school. Bradley had to turn in his book report to Mrs. Ebbel, but he wanted Carla to see it first, just in case he ripped it up.

Carla was wearing a fluffy pink sweater. "I always

156

wondered what happened to the peanuts too," she said.

"Me too," said Bradley. "And they could have hid the elephant in the garage. That's why they put wallpaper there. To cover up the fingerprints!"

"Do elephants have fingerprints?" asked Carla.

"Maybe they have trunk prints." He laughed. "Well, I have to go to Mrs. Ebbel's class. Here's your book back. Thank you. I didn't write on it or spill food or anything."

"I'd like for you to keep it," said Carla. "It's my present to you."

"But I thought it was one of your favorite books?"

"It is. That's why I want to give it to you. If I didn't like it, then it wouldn't be much of a present, would it?"

He smiled. "I wish I had a present to give you," he said.

"You already gave me one."

"I did? What was it?"

"The book report."

The smile left his face.

"What's the matter?"

"Well, I'm supposed to give it to Mrs. Ebbel, but . . . that's okay! You can have it. It wouldn't be much of a present if I didn't want it too."

Carla laughed and shook her head. "That's very sweet, Bradley, but that's not what I meant. I want you to give it to Mrs. Ebbel. It just makes me very happy that you did such a wonderful job. That's the present you gave me."

"Really?"

"Really," said Carla. "It was the best present I could have gotten."

He thought that was great. He was able to give it to Carla and still give it to Mrs. Ebbel. "What's wrong?"

Carla wiped her eyes. The corners of her mouth trembled.

"Are you crying?" he asked.

"Bradley, I have something I have to tell you," she said. "I hope you can listen to what I have to say without feeling scared or upset."

He suddenly felt very scared and upset.

"Tomorrow will be my last day here at Red Hill School."

"Huh?"

"That's why I'm so glad you've written such a wonderful book report. I know you can continue to do good work without me. I'm very proud of you."

"You're leaving?"

She nodded. "I've been transferred. I'll be teaching kindergarten at Willow Bend School. But I want to thank you, Bradley. You've made my short time here very special. I'm so glad we got to know each other."

"You're leaving?"

"We can still see each other," she said. "Saturday, I'm—"

He shook his head. "No, you can't go. It's not fair."

"I have to."

He couldn't believe it. "What if I don't do my homework? Then you'll have to stay and make me want to do it again."

She smiled warmly at him. Her blue eyes glistened. "You're on your own now, Bradley. I know you'll do wonderfully!"

"No! It's not fair!" He stood up. "You tricked me!"

Carla stood too. She walked around the table toward him.

"I hate you!" he shouted in her face.

"I know you don't mean that."

"Yes, I do. I hate your stupid book, too!" He picked up *My Parents Didn't Steal an Elephant* by Uriah C. Lasso and threw it at her. Then he picked up his book report.

"Bradley, please—"

He ripped it in half. He stretched his mouth so wide it was hard to tell whether it was a smile or a frown.

He tore his book report again and dropped the pieces on the floor. "I hate you!" he shouted, then ran out of her office.

He ran into the boys' bathroom. He leaned over the sink and cried. His face throbbed as he watched the water wash down the drain.

There was a knock on the bathroom door. "Bradley?" said Carla. "Are you all right?"

"Go away!" he yelled. "I hate you!"

The door slowly opened and she stepped inside.

"You're not allowed in here," he said.

"I think it's important that we talk," said Carla. "That's how friends handle their problems, by talking about them. That's why we've become such good friends, because we've learned to talk to each other."

"I'm not your friend. Why would I want to be friends with you? I hate you!"

"I like you, Bradley. I can like you, can't I? You don't have to like me."

"I'm not going to Colleen's birthday party," he said. "And I don't like Jeff, either, and I'm never going to do my homework, ever, and I'm going to fail all my tests."

"Do you want to know what I think? I think you're worried that now that I'm leaving, everything will turn bad again. You think that Jeff won't like you anymore and Colleen won't want you to come to her party, and Mrs. Ebbel will give you bad grades no matter how hard you try."

"This is the boys' bathroom!"

"But it wasn't me who magically changed your life, Bradley," she said. "It was you. You're not Cinderella, and I'm not Prince Charming."

"You're not allowed in here," he said coldly.

"Saturday, I'm going to need someone to help me move all my things out of the office," she said. "I would appreciate it very much if you would come and help me. Then afterward, we could have lunch together. We can go to a restaurant, just the two of us."

He wanted to go to her, to hug her in her soft pink sweater, but he couldn't. He felt like his insides were being ripped apart.

"It will be lots of fun," said Carla. "And it would be a great help to me."

"I have to use the toilet."

"Maybe I'll see you on Saturday," said Carla. "I would like that very much." She turned and walked out the door.

Bradley stayed in the bathroom until the bell rang, then he went home, sick.

39.

Ronnie hopped along, singing, "doo de-doo de-doo de-doo."

All the other animals were gathered together.

"What are you doing?" asked Ronnie.

"We're talking," said the lion.

"And you can't listen," said the kangaroo.

"Oh, okay," said Ronnie. She waited for the other animals to finish talking.

The other animals finished talking.

"We finished talking," the lion told Ronnie. "We took a vote. We don't like you anymore."

Ronnie hopped away. Suddenly, she fell into quicksand!

"Help!" she cried. "Bartholomew, save me!"

"No, I won't," said Bartholomew. "And I'm not going to marry you either."

Ronnie sank into the quicksand and died.

40.

Bradley's mother took his temperature and told him he was normal.

"I am not!" he argued.

"He's not normal," Claudia agreed. "He's bizarre."

Bradley felt as if his stomach were tied in a knot. Every time he thought about Carla, he felt the knot pull tighter.

"I hate her! I hate her!" he repeated as he slowly walked to school. When he said he hated her, the knot in his stomach loosened just a little bit.

He sat at his desk in the back of Mrs. Ebbel's room—last seat, last row.

"Hi, Bradley," said Jeff, sitting down next to him. "Where were you yesterday? Were you sick?"

He didn't answer. Jeff wasn't his friend. He didn't have any friends.

"Bradley!" called Mrs. Ebbel. "Will you come here, please?"

He dragged his feet to her desk. "I was sick yesterday," he told her. "Call my mother if you don't believe me."

Mrs. Ebbel waved that away. "I just wanted to tell you how much I enjoyed your book report," she said. "It made me want to read the book."

"Huh?"

"Miss Davis gave it to me yesterday," Mrs. Ebbel told him. "She explained how she accidentally ripped it."

He stared at her, amazed, then noticed his book report, taped together, lying on Mrs. Ebbel's desk. At the very top, in red ink, was the word *Excellent!*

"I gave you a gold star," said Mrs. Ebbel.

He picked up his book report and ran back to his desk.

There it was—next to the name "Bradley Chalkers" —a gold star! He slowly sat down as he stared at it. It seemed to shine brighter than all the other stars.

The knot in his stomach jerked tight and he had to look away. The star reminded him of Carla.

She's such a liar, he thought. *She said she accidentally tore it up when I was the one who did it. I hate her.* He shoved his book report in the back of his desk.

The knot loosened.

He walked all recess. The other boys called to him from the basketball court, but he pretended not to hear them. He just kept walking.

Okay, he decided. *I'll go see her at lunch. I'll just say good-bye to her, that's all.*

"Everyone was looking for you to play basketball," Jeff said when he returned to class. "I told 'em you were still sick from yesterday."

"I'm not sick," said Bradley. "I'm normal."

When the bell rang for lunch, he walked to Mrs. Ebbel's desk to ask for the hall pass.

"Yes, Bradley?" she said.

He couldn't talk. The knot in his stomach was so tight it choked off his vocal cords.

He stuck his hands in his pockets and walked outside. He sat in a far corner of the playground. Twice he thought he saw Carla. The first time it was a third-grade girl. The second time it was a tree. His stomach was too knotted up to eat anything.

"I saw Carla," Jeff told him after lunch. "I went to her office to say good-bye. She said she'd like to see you. She said she'd wait in her office after school for you in case you wanted to talk to her. She asked me to tell you that."

Bradley closed his eyes until the knot loosened.

"Don't you even want to say good-bye to her?" Jeff asked.

He shook his head.

He could picture her waiting in her office for him. He'd walk in and she'd say, "Hello, Bradley. It's a pleasure to see you today. I appreciate your coming to see me." She might even kiss him again.

When the final bell rang, he walked directly home. The knot inside him tightened with every step he took. *I hate her! I hate her! I hate her!*

41.

"Let's go, Bradley!" his mother said on Saturday morning as she entered his room. "We're off to a real barber shop!" She said it as if a barber shop was the most wonderful place in the world.

In the past, she had always cut Bradley's hair herself. But this time he had asked to go to a "real" barber shop. That was earlier in the week, when they were out buying the birthday present for Colleen. "You make my head look like a chili bowl," he had complained.

Now he sadly looked up at his mother and said, "I don't want to get my hair cut."

"You want to look nice for Colleen's birthday party tomorrow, don't you?" she asked. "You don't want to go looking like a punk rocker!"

"I'm not going to her birthday party!" he snapped. "I hate her!"

Bradley's mother left him alone.

He heard Carla's voice in his mind. *Saturday, I'm going to need someone to help me move all my things out of the office. I would appreciate it very much if you would come and help me.*

The knot in his stomach tightened.

"No. I hate you!" he said out loud.

His father knocked, then came into his room.

"Bradley, I think we need to talk," he said, "man to man."

Bradley stood up.

"Why don't you tell me what's bothering you?" asked his father. "Maybe I can help."

Bradley didn't want any help.

"I was very sorry to hear that your counselor had been transferred to another school," said his father. "I know how much you liked her. At first I didn't like the idea of you seeing a counselor, but—"

"I have to get my hair cut," said Bradley. "Mom said so." He walked out of his room, leaving his father behind him.

His mother drove him to the barber shop.

Carla's voice spoke in his mind. *We could have lunch together. We can go to a restaurant.*

The knot pulled tighter.

Just the two of us.

And tighter.

It will be lots of fun, Carla said. *And it would be a great help to me.*

And tighter.

Maybe I'll see you on Saturday, said Carla. *I would like that very much.*

And tighter.

You're not Cinderella, and I'm not Prince Charming.

And tighter.

I like you, Bradley. I can like you, can't I? You don't have to like me.

The knot pulled so tight, it broke. "Stop the car!" he shouted. "I have to go back!"

The car swerved. "Don't ever do that again!" exclaimed his mother. "We could have had an accident."

"I don't believe in accidents."

"I'm getting sick and tired of your nonsense, Bradley. What is your problem?"

"I can't get my hair cut now. I have to go to school."

"On Saturday?"

"I'm supposed to see my counselor. She is waiting to see me. Call the school if you don't believe me."

The car stopped in the parking lot in front of the barber shop. "We're here!" his mother said sternly. "You're getting your hair cut, now."

He stepped out of the car and reluctantly followed his mother into the barber shop.

It smelled oily, like hair and hair oil and stale bubble gum all mixed together. All around him, mirrors reflected mirrors. The place was ugly and the mirrors reflected the ugliness, multiplying it a hundred times back and forth. They seemed to reflect the awful smell too.

He couldn't believe he had asked his mother to take him to such a place. It was like some kind of horrible dungeon where kids went to be tortured. But worst of all, he had to wait his turn to be tortured. All the barber chairs were occupied.

He sat on a torn red couch.

"Do you want to read a comic book?" asked his mother.

"No thank you," he answered quietly.

Finally, it was his turn. He climbed into a slippery, oily, vinyl barber chair. The barber tied a shiny apron tightly around his neck, nearly choking him to death.

The barber began by combing his hair. Bradley wondered why he had to comb it if he was going to cut it anyway.

At last, the barber picked up the scissors and began to cut. But he never cut off a big piece of hair all at once. Instead he kept snipping little bits of hair off of the same piece of hair, over and over again. The whole time, Bradley had to stare at himself through the filmy mirror. He gritted his teeth and waited for it to be over.

The barber put down the scissors, but then he picked up the comb and started combing again.

I knew he shouldn't have combed it before, Bradley thought. *Now he just has to do it again.*

The barber sprayed some kind of smelly junk on Bradley's head, combed his hair one last time, then unhooked the apron around Bradley's neck.

Bradley quickly hopped off the chair before the barber could change his mind.

But the barber wasn't through. He made Bradley stand still while he ran a small vacuum cleaner across his neck. When he finished, he offered Bradley a piece of bubble gum.

"I hate gum," said Bradley. He never used to hate

gum. But after smelling it in the barber shop, he never wanted another piece again.

"You'll be the most handsome boy at Colleen's party," his mother said as they walked outside.

"Can you drive me to school, please?" he asked. She nodded.

Ten minutes later he jumped out of the car, ran up the steps in front of the school, and pulled on the double glass doors. They were locked. He pressed his face against the glass and looked inside. Mrs. Kemp, the janitor, was waxing the floors. He pounded on the door until she looked up.

Mrs. Kemp scowled at him as she opened the door. "What do you want, Chalkers?"

"I have to see Car— Miss Davis," he said.

"Miss Davis is gone."

He ducked under her arm which held open the door, and ran into the building.

"Chalkers!" she shouted after him. "I'll call the police!"

He opened the door to Carla's office and stepped inside. Except for the round table and chairs, the room was empty. But in his mind he heard Carla say, *Hello, Bradley. It's a pleasure to see you today. I appreciate your coming to see me.*

Tears rolled down his face.

He noticed a large manila envelope lying on the table. He picked it up.

BRADLEY CHALKERS was written across it in big letters. Under that, in smaller letters, was the following:

170

Mrs. Ebbel's class
Room 12
Good friend,
Honest,
Thoughtful,
Caring,
Polite,
Whom I will never forget,
And who I hope
Will someday
Forgive me
Last seat, last row

"There you are!" said Mrs. Kemp as she came in after him. "If you don't get out of here right now, I'm going to call the police."

"Look!" he exclaimed, holding up the envelope. "She left this for me. See! We were friends. Carla and me. We were best friends."

"You have ten seconds to leave this building," said Mrs. Kemp. "One . . . two . . ."

He took the envelope and left.

He opened it on the playground, next to the monkey bars. Inside was the book *My Parents Didn't Steal an Elephant*, by Uriah C. Lasso, and a letter.

Dear Bradley,

This book was a present from me to you. It was a gift from the heart, and that kind of gift, for better or worse, can never be returned.

I'm sorry for hurting you. I didn't mean to. If it

makes you feel any better, you hurt me, too, when you didn't come see me Friday or Saturday. I kept hoping I'd see your happy face walk through the door.

I hope you didn't mind that I gave your book report to Mrs. Ebbel. It was just too good to throw away. You can do such wonderful work. Now, if only you can learn how not to rip it up.

I hope you went to Colleen's birthday party. If you did, I'm sure you enjoyed it. If you didn't go, that's all right too. There will be lots of other parties. You're a very likable person. You'll always be very special to me.

It was always a pleasure to see you. I appreciated your coming to see me. Thank you for sharing so much with me.

I love you,
Carla

Bradley's father was leaning on his cane, on the front stoop, when Bradley came walking home. "I want to talk to you, Bradley," he said sternly.

Bradley ran to him and hugged him, nearly knocking him over.

42.

Bradley tried writing a letter to Carla. His father had suggested it. He crumpled up a piece of paper and threw it in his wastepaper basket. He didn't know what to say to her. The words he wanted hadn't been invented yet.

Ronnie hopped along, singing, "doo de-doo de-doo de-doo."

The other animals were taking another vote.

"We took another vote," the lion told Ronnie. "We like you the best."

"I like all of you the best too," said Ronnie.

Bartholomew walked up to her. "I love you, Ronnie," he said. "Will you marry me?"

"Yes," said Ronnie.

"And I saved you from the quicksand too," said Bartholomew, "so you didn't die."

"That's good," said Ronnie. "I'm very glad to hear that."

43.

Colleen, wearing a new red dress, anxiously waited for her guests to arrive. Except for Lori and Melinda, she hadn't told anybody that there would be *boys* at her party.

The doorbell rang.

Her heart jumped. She hoped it would be Jeff and also hoped it wouldn't be. She composed herself and opened the door.

It was Judy and Betty. They each gave her a present. "Ooh, what is it?" Colleen asked as she took each gift, but of course they didn't tell her.

"Who else is coming?" asked Judy as the three girls sat and waited in the living room.

Colleen counted on her fingers, naming her guests. "Well, there's you two, and Lori and Melinda, Karen, Amie and Dena . . ." She paused, then said the last two names very quickly, "andJeffandBradley."

"Bradley?" questioned Betty. "Bradley Chalkers? Oh, no!"

Judy looked like she was about to faint.

"You didn't say there were going to be boys at your party," said Betty.

"Didn't I?" Colleen asked innocently. "I thought I did."

"I don't think I'm allowed to go to a boy and girl party," said Judy.

"Okay, but you already gave me my present," said Colleen.

They decided to stay. When the bell rang again, all three girls screamed, but it was only Amie and Dena.

Amie and Dena were dressed exactly alike, right down to their shoes and socks. They were best friends and their parents often took them shopping together. They always bought the same clothes. Then, before a party, or even just before school sometimes, they'd call each other up and decide what to wear. Today it was a blue dress with white-and-yellow flowery things.

"Colleen invited boys!" Betty told them.

"Bradley Chalkers!" said Judy.

Amie and Dena looked at each other in horror. Colleen took their presents from them, before they could change their minds. Both presents were wrapped in the same purple-and-green paper.

Karen was the next to arrive. "Colleen invited boys!" everyone said to her as she stood in the doorway.

Her mouth dropped open.

"Bradley Chalkers," said Betty.

"And the new kid," said Amie. "Jeff Fishfood."

Karen was very shy and quiet. If there were going to be boys at the party, she might not say one word all day.

The doorbell rang. Everyone except Karen screamed. She held a pillow in front of her face.

It was Lori and Melinda.

"Colleen invited boys!" everyone greeted them.

"Jeff Fishnose and *Bradley Chalkers*," said Dena.

"So, we already knew that," Lori said, as if it were no big deal to her.

"Oh, well, nobody else did," said Judy.

The eight girls waited. They talked and laughed about how much Colleen would like her presents. They asked her what there would be to eat and what games they would play. The one thing they didn't talk about was *boys*, though it was the only thing on each of their minds.

When Colleen told Dena there would be a three-legged race, the room turned very quiet. Each girl wondered if she would have to run it with a boy.

Colleen planned to run the three-legged race with Jeff. It didn't occur to her that if she was partners with Jeff, another girl would have to be partners with Bradley.

It was starting to get late. A new worry slowly crept into each girl's head. *What if the boys didn't show up?* It suddenly seemed that the party wouldn't be any fun at all without boys. *Where were they?*

Colleen's mother walked into the living room and counted heads. "Eight," she said aloud. "Who's missing?"

Nobody answered.

"Oh, the boys," said Colleen's mother. "Well, we can't wait too much longer."

Colleen looked like she was about to cry.

Where were they?

44.

The doorbell rang at Bradley's house.

Bradley, wearing a cone-shaped party hat, ran to the front door and flung it open. He had a wild look in his eyes.

"Hi," said Jeff, holding Colleen's present under his arm. "You ready?" He was wearing old, comfortable clothes. His blue jeans had a small hole above the knee.

"It's wrapped!" Bradley exclaimed. "With a bow!"

"Wha—?" uttered Jeff.

Bradley ran back to his parents' bedroom. "It's got to be wrapped!" he told his mother. "With a bow!"

She cut off a piece of tape and smiled at her son. "I'm wrapping it now."

"Okay, good!" He returned to the front door. "My mother's wrapping it now," he told Jeff.

He had been running around the house that way all morning as he desperately tried to get ready for the birthday party. He'd already changed his clothes six times. He didn't know what he was supposed to wear. He didn't know what he was supposed to do. He didn't know what he didn't know!

Claudia had given him the party hat to wear. She told him he wasn't allowed to take it off.

"They wrapped my present at the store where I got it," Jeff said.

Bradley hardly heard him. "Are you supposed to wear torn pants?" he asked.

"What?"

He ran into the kitchen. He took a sharp knife from the drawer next to the sink and cut a hole in his pants, just above the knee.

When he returned to the front door, Jeff was standing inside the house. Claudia was with him. "Is my hat on straight?" Bradley asked his sister.

She looked him over. "It's hard to tell," she explained, "because your head's crooked."

Mrs. Chalkers came down the hall holding Colleen's present in front of her. "See, all wrapped," she said. "Hello, you must be Jeff. I'm Bradley's mother."

"Hello, Mrs. Chalkers," said Jeff.

"It doesn't have a bow!" Bradley shouted.

"Oh, I couldn't find any ribbon," said his mother.

He stared at her in disbelief. "It needs a bow!" he wailed. He turned to Jeff. "Doesn't it need a bow?"

"No."

"Oh, okay," he said happily. He took the present from his mother. She kissed him and told him to have fun.

He and Jeff started out the door.

"Oh, Bradley," said his mother, "you ripped your pants."

"I know." He closed the door.

They headed up the sidewalk toward Colleen's. She lived two blocks away.

"Do you want my bow?" Jeff asked. "I can take it off."

Bradley nervously shook his head.

"Are you all right?" Jeff asked.

"Umukum," said Bradley. He had tried to say "I'm okay," but his mouth didn't work.

"You're acting kind of strange," said Jeff, "even for you, I mean."

Bradley sighed and stopped walking.

"What's the matter?" Jeff asked.

Bradley trembled. He felt the same way as when he first tried to turn in his homework. "I don't know what to do at a birthday party," he said, shivering.

Jeff laughed.

Bradley sat down on the curb. "I haven't been to one in three years!"

Jeff looked impatiently up the street, then sat down next to his best friend. "There's nothing to worry about," he said assuringly. "Birthday parties are fun."

"How many birthday parties have you been to?" Bradley asked.

Jeff shrugged. "A lot. What do you want to know?"

"Everything."

"Okay," said Jeff. "First take off that dumb hat!"

So, while the eight girls anxiously waited, Jeff was patiently trying to teach Bradley everything he knew about birthday parties.

45.

Bradley watched Jeff poke his finger into the doorbell and heard it ring inside the house. Then there was a loud scream. A moment later Colleen opened the door.

"Hap-py birthd—" he sang, but stopped when Jeff elbowed him in his side.

"This is for you," Jeff said, handing Colleen his present.

"This is for you," said Bradley as he did the same.

"Ooh, what is it?" she asked.

"It's a—" Bradley started, but Jeff elbowed him again, so he shut his mouth. They followed Colleen into the house.

"You're not supposed to tell her what you got her," Jeff whispered.

"But she asked."

"She's supposed to ask. But you're not supposed to tell her. Don't tell *anyone*."

Bradley nodded like he understood, but of course he didn't.

"Hello, Bradley," said Melinda.

He looked to Jeff for help.

"Hello, Melinda," said Jeff.

"Hello, Melinda," said Bradley.

Colleen's mother came in and led everyone out to the backyard. A picnic table had been set up on the patio with paper plates and cups. Bradley chose a seat and sat down.

"My, this boy must be hungry!" said Colleen's mother.

The girls laughed.

Bradley looked around, puzzled. He was the only one sitting down. He quickly rose, bumping against the table. A paper cup fell onto the ground. As he bent down to pick it up, he knocked over his chair.

The girls were hysterical. Bradley looked around helplessly. Amie picked up the cup and Dena set the chair right.

"We don't eat yet," Jeff explained as Bradley made it safely away from the table. "First we have to play games."

Bradley turned pale.

"Just do whatever I do," said Jeff.

A large dog dashed out through the back door and jumped up on Bradley, putting his muddy paws on his clean shirt. Bradley nearly fell over.

"Chicken, get down!" scolded Colleen's mother.

Chicken had wiry red hair and a square face. He got down, but stayed by Bradley's side.

"Chicken's usually afraid of everybody," said Colleen.

Bradley patted his head, glad Chicken liked him.

Mrs. Verigold split the group into two teams for a relay race. She put Jeff and Bradley on separate teams because she said it wouldn't be fair for the two boys to be together.

Bradley lined up with the other members of his

team. He was in the middle. Amie and Betty were in front of him. Judy and Dena were behind him.

On the other team, Jeff was talking to Colleen. Bradley wondered if he should talk to one of the girls on his team, but he didn't know what to say. Besides, they were all talking to each other. He petted Chicken.

"On your mark," said Mrs. Verigold, "get set . . . *go!*"

Suddenly the race started and everyone on his team was screaming. "C'mon, Amie!" "Go!" "Run, Amie!" "Faster!"

He watched Amie run and touch a tree at the end of the yard, then turn around and come back. She slapped Betty's hand, then Betty ran toward the tree.

"Run, Betty!" everyone except Bradley shouted. "Slow down, Betty," he whispered to himself, hoping his turn would never come.

He turned around. Judy was behind him, yelling to Betty. "Do you want to go next?" he asked her.

"Stick your hand out!" she hollered back.

He spun around and stuck his hand out just in time. Betty slapped it and he took off. He ran as hard as he could to the tree.

"Go, Bradley!" he heard someone yell. "C'mon, Bradley!" It made him want to run faster than he'd ever run before. Chicken barked at his side.

Melinda was running for the other team. She had started before him, but he beat her to the tree. He almost slipped and fell, but caught his balance and charged back toward his cheering teammates.

"C'mon, Bradley!" they all yelled.

He slapped Judy's hand, then bent over to catch his breath. He turned and shouted louder than anyone, "Go, Judy! Run!" then, "C'mon, Dena!"

Dena crossed the finish line and everyone on his team jumped up and down.

"What happened?" he asked.

"We won!" said Betty.

He jumped up and down too.

"That means we each get two points," said Judy.

That was something new. Jeff hadn't told him anything about points.

Judy explained it to him. "Everybody on the winning team gets two points, and everybody on the losing team gets one point."

Betty interrupted. "It would come out the same if they just gave one point to the winners and nothing to the losers," she said, "but this way the losers don't feel as bad."

"*I'm* telling him!" said Judy. "After each race we trade teams, and then at the end of all the races, Colleen's mother counts up the points and the girl with the most points gets first pick from the basket of prizes. Then the girl with the second most gets second pick, and so on."

"Colleen's mother has a chart with everyone's name on it to keep track of the points," explained Betty.

"I'm telling him!" said Judy. "Colleen's mother has a chart."

Bradley laughed with delight. "Are all birthday parties this much fun?" he asked.

Judy and Betty looked at each other. The only thing that made this party special was *the boys*, but they couldn't tell that to Bradley.

"Haven't you ever been to a birthday party before?" asked Betty.

"Not for a long time. I got kicked out of the last one I went to."

"Well, if you have any questions, just ask me," said Betty.

"Or me," said Judy.

"I've been to more birthday parties than you," said Betty.

"You have not!" said Judy. "She hasn't."

"What about Holly's birthday party?" asked Betty. "You didn't go to that one."

"That's because we were on vacation," said Judy.

"So, you still didn't go."

They had to switch teams for the next relay race. This time Bradley was with Betty, Amie, Karen, and Melinda. For this race, everyone had to hop on one foot.

"On one foot!" Bradley exclaimed.

He rooted loudly for everyone on his team, and when it was his turn, he heard them all cheer for him. His team won again.

"You're an excellent hopper, Melinda," he said

after the race. "You hopped twice as far as Colleen on each hop."

Melinda beamed. "You're a good hopper too," she said.

Colleen's mother marked the points on the chart, and they switched teams for the next race. This time they had to hop on both feet.

"On both feet!" Bradley exclaimed.

They continued changing teams for each new race. He and Jeff were never allowed on the same team, and since Colleen always made sure that she was on Jeff's team, Bradley was never with her either.

He was glad about that. He felt comfortable with everybody else, but he was still a little scared of Colleen. He was afraid she might ask him another question he wasn't supposed to answer.

Lori was on his team for the backward race. She stood behind him in line and screamed in his ear the whole time. He loved it. He had to shout twice as loud just to hear himself.

His ear was still ringing when Mrs. Verigold announced that the next race would be a somersault race.

The smile left his face. He didn't know how to do a somersault! He looked anxiously at Chicken.

But as it turned out, nobody on his team could do a somersault! It was hilarious. Everyone was laughing. When it was his turn, he rolled and flopped in every direction except the way he was supposed to go. And every time he hit the ground, Chicken tried to lick his face. Perhaps he would have done better if he could have stopped laughing.

Everybody on the other team was good at somersaults. The teams just worked out that way. Karen was the best.

"You should be in the Olympics!" he told her after the race.

She smiled and blushed.

Bradley smiled too. Even though his team lost, he thought it had been the most fun race of the day.

Plus, when the girls somersaulted in their party dresses, he could see their underwear.

46.

Colleen's mother told everyone to find a partner for the three-legged race. Jeff and Colleen looked nervously at each other.

Judy and Betty paired up. They stood side by side with their arms around each other's shoulders as Mrs. Verigold tied their inside legs together.

Lori and Melinda became another team. Bradley thought they looked funny since Melinda was almost twice Lori's size.

Amie and Dena looked even funnier. Since they were both dressed the same, they looked like a two-headed monster. Except, of course, he didn't believe in monsters.

Karen suddenly realized what was happening. If Jeff and Colleen became partners, it meant she'd have to be partners with Bradley!

"So, um," Jeff said to Colleen. "Who's your partner?"

"No one, yet," said Colleen. "Who's yours?"

"No one, yet."

Colleen's mother stepped in and paired up the final two teams. She didn't think it would be proper for a boy and a girl to have their legs tied together, so she made Jeff and Bradley one team, and Colleen and Karen the other.

Bradley was glad that he and Jeff were finally on the same team. Colleen and Jeff were happy with the teams too. As much as they liked each other, they weren't quite ready to put their arms around each other and tie their legs together. Karen was the only one who was disappointed. She thought it would have been exciting to have been partners with Bradley.

The five teams lined up. It wasn't a relay race. Each team would go at the same time. They had to run past the tree to the fence, then back.

"Don't try to run too fast," Jeff cautioned. "The most important thing is that we keep together so we don't fall down."

Bradley nodded.

"On your mark," said Mrs. Verigold. "Get set . . . go!"

They took two steps, then tumbled to the ground.

As they tried to get up, they kept pulling each other back down. At last they stood up together and started after the others.

"Inside, outside, inside, outside . . ." Jeff directed as they moved their legs in unison.

The other teams took a long time turning around at the fence. When Jeff and Bradley reached the fence, they simply fell down again and stood up facing the other direction. It was quicker that way.

Amie and Dena were just ahead of them. Amie tried to go to the left of the tree as Dena tried to go to the right of it. They smashed into it.

"Inside, outside, inside, outside . . ." said Jeff as he and Bradley charged around them.

Karen and Colleen were in the lead when they suddenly stumbled and fell on their faces. Judy and Betty tumbled over them.

Lori and Melinda had to stop and turn to avoid the pile.

Jeff and Bradley charged past, now in first place. "Inside, outside, inside, outside . . ." called Jeff, but they must have missed a beat somewhere because when he said, "Inside," they moved their outside feet, and when he said, "Outside," they moved their inside feet.

"Hey, Bradley, you're going the wrong way!" yelled Lori.

"Whoa, ahhh blbph!"

Amie and Dena dived across the finish line in first place, just ahead of Lori and Melinda. Jeff and Bradley crawled across in third. Judy, Betty, Karen, and Colleen remained tangled together on the grass.

After everyone got untied, they gathered on the grass next to the patio. "Now what?" Bradley asked nobody in particular.

"Colleen's mother is adding up the points," said Betty.

"Then we'll get to pick our prizes," said Judy.

"He asked *me!*" said Betty.

Everyone hushed as Mrs. Verigold prepared to announce the winner. "The winner is . . ."—she paused suspensefully—". . . Bradley!"

He was shocked. He had been on the winning team every time except for the three-legged race and the somersault race, but he had been having too much fun to notice.

Everyone clapped their hands as he walked to the front. Mrs. Verigold gave him a blue ribbon that said First Place on it. No one had told him about the ribbon. Then he got to pick a prize.

He looked through the basket. There were lots of good things from which to choose: dolls, makeup, perfume, earrings, hair ornaments. He chose a harmonica.

Melinda came in second. Then Amie, Judy, Dena, Karen, Lori, and Betty, and Jeff was last.

Jeff knew he'd be last, since he was never on Bradley's team. The only race he won was the somersault race. Actually, he had tied for last with Colleen, but Colleen didn't get a prize because she'd be getting all her presents later.

Jeff took the only prize left in the basket, a doll's dress. "Thank you," he said politely.

"Now what?" Bradley asked.

"We have ice cream and cake," said Melinda.

"Oh boy," said Bradley.

Melinda laughed.

They sat at the picnic table. Colleen sat at the head of the table. Bradley sat between Jeff and Melinda. Judy and Betty sat across from him.

"Mrs. Verigold's going to bring in the cake now," said Judy.

"With candles," said Betty.

"I'm telling him!" said Judy. "With candles."

Mrs. Verigold brought in the cake and suddenly everyone started singing. Bradley was caught by surprise. He didn't have time to remember the words, though he tried. He sang:

> *Hap-py birth-day dear Col— to you.*
> *Hap-py birth-day to you.*
> *Hap-py birth-day to y— Dear Colleen,*
> *Hap-py birth-day dea— to you,*
> *Hap-py birth-day to—"*

He suddenly realized he was the only one still singing.

Everyone laughed.

"It's not his fault," said Judy. "This is his first birthday party in a long time."

"There are ten candles because she's ten years old," explained Betty.

"Oh, I get it!" said Bradley.

Lori laughed.

Colleen blew them all out.

"That means her wish will come true," explained Melinda.

"But she can't tell you what she wished for, otherwise it won't come true," Lori explained.

Bradley carefully ate his cake and ice cream, without making a mess. Then everyone went into the living room, where Colleen opened her presents.

"Open mine!" "Mine first," they urged. "That one's mine!"

"Open mine, Colleen," said Bradley.

After each present was opened, everyone said, "How neat," and "Ooh," and "I wish I had one of those."

Bradley said those things too, and he meant what he said, although most of the gifts were things he never would have wanted.

Colleen picked up the next present.

"That's mine!" he shouted.

Colleen read the card. On the front of the card there was a picture of a baseball player swinging a baseball bat. It said, "Here's hoping your birthday is . . ." On the inside of the card it showed the bat smacking a ball and it said, "a big hit!" Under that it said, "Happy Birthday," and it was signed, *Love, Bradley*.

Everyone went crazy. "Love!" exclaimed Amie. "Love?"

Bradley's heart sank as he realized he had made a terrible mistake.

"Bradley's in love with Colleen!" said Dena.

"Oooh, Bradley," said Judy.

"When are you getting married?" teased Lori.

"Shut up!" Karen shouted.

Everyone stopped talking and looked at her very surprised.

"*Big* deal!" said Karen. "You're all so immature."

Colleen tore off the wrapping paper and looked at Bradley's gift. Her mouth dropped open. She showed it to everyone.

"Wow!" said Lori.

"Let me see!" said Amie.

It was a replica of the human heart. They could see all the blood vessels, the aorta, and all the capillaries. The heart valves opened and shut. It could be taken apart and put back together again.

"How neat!" said Melinda.

"I wish I had one of those," said Betty.

Bradley smiled proudly. He felt happier about the fact that Colleen liked his present than about coming in first place. But, of course, he knew all along she'd like it. Carla had told him to give her a gift from the heart.

Colleen opened the rest of the presents, then everyone went home.

Jeff and Bradley left together. It was still light outside, although the street lights had come on.

"So?" asked Jeff.

"Wasn't that fun!" Bradley exclaimed. "It was the most, at first when I gave Colleen her present and she asked me what it was, I almost told her! And then when I was the only one sitting at the table, 'My this boy must be hungry,' but then the races started and everyone got points, even the losers. Only next time I won't sign it *love*. Karen's a good somersaulter. Chicken's a funny name for a dog. Maybe if they get a chicken, they'll name it Dog!"

He blew into his harmonica.

The doll's dress dangled from Jeff's hand.

47.

Dear Carla,

Hi. What color shirt are you wearing today? I'm sorry I yelled at you. Guess what? I got a hundred percent on my arithmetic test. Can you believe it? And I didn't rip it up! I would have sent it to you, but I can't because it's hanging on a wall in Mrs. Ebbel's class. Do you like teaching kindergarten? I bet you're a good teacher. Ask them to draw pictures for you. You should teach them how to do somersaults, too. Thanks for giving me back the book which you already gave me. I'm sending you a present too. It's a gift from the heart, so you can't return it.

~~Love,~~
~~Yours truly,~~
Love,
Bradley

P.S. Her name is Ronnie.

Bradley folded the letter and put it in the envelope. He wrote Carla's name on the outside and addressed it to Willow Bend School.

Ronnie gave Bartholomew a big hug and kiss.

"Well, good-bye everybody," she said.

"Good-bye, Ronnie," said everybody.

"I'll miss you," said Bartholomew.

Bradley placed the little red rabbit with the broken ear inside the envelope.

He stared out his window for a moment, then looked back down at the bulge in the envelope. He frowned. But it was an unusual frown. In fact, it might have been a smile.

LOUIS SACHAR

holes

BLOOMSBURY

Nominated for the Carnegie Medal 2011

The Cardturner

From the bestselling author of HOLES

louis sachar

'You don't notice the daredevil artistry of his storytelling until it's too late ... As Uncle Lester might say, nicely played, Louis'

Frank Cottrell Boyce, Guardian

AVAILABLE NOW

About the author

LOUIS SACHAR is the author of the New York Times number one bestseller *Holes*, winner of the Newbery Medal, the National Book Award and the Christopher Award. He is also the author of *Fuzzy Mud*; *Stanley Yelnats' Survival Guide to Camp Green Lake*; *Small Steps*, winner of the Schneider Family Book Award; and *The Cardturner*, a Publishers Weekly Best Book, a Parents' Choice Gold Award recipient, and an ALA-YALSA Best Fiction for Young Adults book. His books for younger readers include *The Boy Who Lost His Face*, *Dogs Don't Tell Jokes*, and the *Marvin Redpost* series, among many others.